Space Marine Ajax

Extinction Fleet

Sean-Michael Argo

Published by Sean-Michael Argo, 2023.

SPACE MARINE AJAX

Extinction Fleet

Book 1

By Sean-Michael Argo

Also by Sean-Michael Argo

Extinction Fleet
Space Marine Ajax

Starwing Elite
Alpha Lance

Standalone
War Machines
DinoMechs: Battle Force Jurassic

Edited by T.L. Bland

Thruterryseyes.com

Table of Contents

FAREWELL PROUD MEN

"Each day in Valhalla they don their war-gear and go down to battle; then do rise again whole in the night to drink mead and eat their fill of meat. Of these einherjar there are many, and yet there will seem too few when the wolf comes." – Prose Edda of Snorri Sturlson circa 1220.

The Garm, as they came to be called, emerged from the deepest parts of uncharted space, devouring all that lay before them, a great swarm that scoured entire star systems of all organic life. This space borne hive, this extinction fleet, made no attempts to communicate and offered no mercy. Such was the ferocity of their assault upon the civilization of humanity that our own wars and schemes were made petty in comparison.

Humanity has always been a deadly organism, and we would not so easily be made the prey. Unified against a common enemy, we fought back, meeting the swarm with soldiers upon every front.

We were resplendent in our fury, and yet, despite the terrible slaughter we visited upon the enemy, world after world still fell beneath ravenous tooth and wicked claw. For every beast slain in the field, another was swiftly hatched to take its place and humanity was faced with a grim war of attrition.

After a decade of bitter galactic conflict, it was all humanity could to do slow the advance of the swarm and with each passing year we came closer to extinction.

The grinding cost of war mounted. The realization set in that without a radical shift in tactics and technology the forces of humanity would run out of soldiers before it ran out of bullets.

In desperate response to the real threat of total annihilation, humanity created the Einherjar. Fearless new warriors with frightening new weapons who were sent to fight the wolves at the gate.

TRENCH 16

The recon scouts had not returned and the defenders were instead met with an enemy force.

"*Spores incoming!*" bellowed the Watchman from his elevated vantage point on the hill just behind the earthen network of trenches. "Swarm advancing!"

Ajax cranked the knob of his respirator to maximum filtration the moment he heard the call, the training of countless artillery drills and endless hours of combat had made the action second nature to him. He then ejected the carbon magazine from his pulse rifle and tapped it against his helmet, settling the inert ammunition firmly in the casing, though functionally, it was more of a pre-battle ritual than a necessary action.

The marine thumbed the activator on the rifle and the weapon snarled to life in his hands, the unique sound of it echoing through the trench as dozens of other marines engaged in similar rituals.

After so many years of war, each soldier on the field had developed their own little ways of preparing for impending combat, each of their individual practices ending in the activation of their rifles.

The combined sound of so many weapons coming online was thrilling. Every soldier in Trench 16 felt the adrenaline pounding through their systems as they heard it. It was the sound of strength, of the power to take life, a burning fire in their hands to keep away the darkness that surged towards them.

With it ringing in his ears, Ajax found that he was not afraid. The marines were strong in their numbers, their weapons deadly in effect, and they held the high ground. In the back of his mind he knew that the horrific beasts that the marines had taken to calling ridgebacks were out there in the night, along with many other terrors, all of which wanted nothing more than to kill and consume every scrap of organic material on this pitiful forgotten planet. Ajax flexed

4

his armored fingers around the grip of the rifle and took a slow, deep breath, knowing it would be the last easy one he'd have for a long while.

The other marines of Hydra Company that defended Trench 16 were taking up their fighting positions throughout the network. Most of them were rifles, like Ajax, though of the two hundred and fifty soldiers in the unit, there were several grenadiers as well.

One of the grenadiers, a man named Boone, stood next to Ajax on the right, his back against the reinforced dirt wall, tapping his fingers against the revolving cylinder of his ordinance launcher.

Rama, another rifle, climbed up from the bottom of the trench to join the other marines on the firing step near the top of the position.

"The Watchman has a keen eye tonight, usually we don't have this much warning before impact," observed Rama as he planted his feet and held his rifle to his shoulder, setting the wide-barrel on the shooting rest at the top of the trench so that he could crank the knob of his helmet's filter. "We might get out of this brawl without any ragmen coming back to haunt us."

"Your optimism is astounding, Rama," snorted Boone. "There are always ragmen, but the warning did go up well in advance of impact, maybe there'll just be a few this time."

"Maybe the ridgebacks ate something that didn't agree with them," Ajax added with a hollow laugh. "Could be that the Watchman saw a muzzle flash."

The marines shared a brief laugh, but were soon interrupted by the familiar whistling sound of incoming spores.

"Brace!" shouted the voices of several marines across the watch channel, and a moment later the first of the spores reached the trench.

There were LED stakes embedded in the ground and on the reinforced walls of the trench, giving enough ambient light for the marines to occupy their position without spotlighting any targets for the enemy that lurked in the darkness at the edges of the perimeter.

In the low light of the stakes, Ajax could see the semi-solid spore streak down from the sky and strike the trench wall opposite the marine.

The Garm ordinance was more like a hardened sack that was ejected with tremendous force from a barrel-like orifice that jutted up from the spine of the ridgebacks. When the sack struck the wall, it burst apart, spewing its contents in all directions.

The spores reminded Ajax of the heavy mists he had experienced in his youth, in some far away country on distant Earth. The spore cloud filled the trench but the marines had enough warning to crank their filters so the spores could only cling to the armor of the marines in hopes of a breach.

More landed around them and Ajax took note of how heavily the enemy bombarded them. It was as if the enemy knew that the marines had prepared for the onslaught and were attempting to make up for that fact by doubling the sheer volume of artillery fire.

The thought of artillery made Ajax cast his gaze across the hill behind the trench. The Watch Tower was a menacing gun battery that rested inside an armored bunker that had been half-buried in the loamy soil. Rising from just behind the quad-barreled artillery piece was the observation post, an elevated capsule that allowed the Watchman to see the full field, even if he was doing so at some risk, given his exposure.

In the low light, it was difficult to make out exactly what was happening at the Tower, but Ajax could tell that the bulk of the spores were smashing into the ground behind the trench.

"Seems like they're more worried about the battery than us," pointed out Ajax as Rama and Boone followed his gaze. "Could be that a shrieker swarm is on the way."

"If that's true, then the Garm would have had to learn the difference between anti-armor and anti-air weapons, not to mention have a forward observer in position to make the distinction," growled Boone before turning back to face the other direction.

"Not even they have a way of piercing this gloom. Why humanity settled any of the brackenworlds in this sector I'll never understand."

Ajax was inclined to agree with Boone, and as more spores pounded the trench and the battery, he strained his eyes in vain to see through the palpable darkness ahead of him.

Brackenworlds were second-rate planets that only warranted partial terra-forming and most of them had similar atmospheric conditions to what the marines were even now experiencing. Marginal light from a distant star that was mostly dissipated by the particle clogged atmosphere, unforgiving landscapes, and only sparse pockets of organic life that rose from the brackish and often fetid water that gave such planets their name.

The modest outpost city of Heorot was the only real sign of civilization on the planet that shared its name, home to only forty thousand souls. They farmed energy, using large windmills to take advantage of the fetid winds the constantly scoured the planet's surface.

It was a testament, really, thought Ajax, that humanity could find something of use even on this backwater world. The planet had little tactical significance, being on the edge of charted space and well removed from the bulk of the besieged human star systems.

A single hive ship had broken off from the main thrust of the extinction fleet and come to terrorize Heorot. The modest city was still a human settlement, carved out of the wilderness by courageous pioneers, so it was worth defending.

A single warship, the Bright Lance, had been sent by Command to counter the enemy, bearing in its hold a legion of Einherjar. A brief star fight had delayed the hive ship's arrival, giving the Einherjar a chance to make planetfall first and prepare their defenses.

There were now twenty gun batteries that defended the city, each with their own trench networks, meaning that just over five thousand marines had put themselves in the path of the enemy.

The Watch Tower, positioned at a vantage point over the whole of the battlefield, was meant to harass any enemy flier formations that attempted to flank the main Einherjar forces that defended the city.

Hydra Company was in place to protect the Tower from any ground swarms that might appear, though Command expected most of the enemy to take the bait and march right into the teeth of Armor One.

The long war against the Garm had left the forces of humanity with limited battle tanks in operation. There were only a few dozen mechanized war machines that comprised the fighting unit.

Ajax hoped they would be enough to combat the ultra-Garm, horrific creatures that served as the battle tank equivalent for the swarm.

The Garm were known, as a fighting force, to attack the strongest point of any defensive position. It was behavior quite unlike the average predator organisms known to humanity, which tended to attack the sick, weak, old, and alone first. However, as the war with the swarm ground onwards, the forces of humanity began to understand the Garm strategy, and it was a troubling discovery indeed.

It was a psychological ploy, one meant to rob the morale of humanity's warriors by destroying their best forces at the outset of any battle. In many ways, by killing the strongest prey first, these nightmare predators made it all the easier to mop up the rest of their prey, who were often at a loss tactically without their leader and demoralized by the destruction of their mightiest champions.

The flash of plasma discharges shone from in and around the battery, and Ajax felt his heart skip a beat, as he realized that it could only mean one thing. At least some of the spores had hit their mark, and even now ragmen were causing havoc for the battery crews. He hoped that his comrades could fend them off, else the guns would be deafeningly silent when the swarm broke against the trench.

"First wave!" boomed the voice of the Watchman, a welcome sound that indicated that he had not been overcome. "Flares up!"

Rama pulled a flare tube from his belt and pressed the ignition as he pointed it at the sky. The brilliant round streaked upwards, illuminating much of the area around the marines. Dozens of others joined it as soldiers up and down the line fired their own flares.

At first, the rounds rose as expected, though instead of reaching their apex and arcing across the battlefield to illuminate the killing ground in front of the trench, many of them were stopped in midair by hundreds of alien bodies.

Focused artillery fire against an anti-air battery, in advance of an aerial assault, it was simply too complex a maneuver for the Garm, and for a moment Ajax refused to believe what he was seeing.

The shriekers, like the rest of the myriad lifeforms that comprised the Garm swarms, looked like a cross between the lizards and cockroaches of distant Earth, if each had been the most nightmarish of its kind. They had the bleak countenance and powerfully muscled bodies of reptiles, but were covered in mucus lubricated sections of chitonous exoskeleton. In their clawed hands most of them carried weapons reminiscent of firearms, though each of them was attached to umbilical cords that connected to pulsing glands under their leathery wings.

There were so many hundreds of them that when the flares struck them, it turned the night sky into a burning tapestry of carnage. Shriekers fell screaming from the sky as holes were burned through their wings. Those slain by the searing hot flares simply plummeting to the ground in silence.

In the glare of the light, Ajax could see their dull black eyes, each one a seeming abyss of hive intelligence and relentless biological automation. To witness such a primal hunger in so many deadly and nightmarish creatures would surely have sent any other group of soldiers to their knees, yet the marines of Hydra Company stood their ground.

Many times, each man among them had faced such horror. The days of collapsing and retching in fear were far behind them. Instead, they raised their rifles and began to fire as the swarm descended upon them, each of the Garm weapons spitting death as they dove at the marines.

Ajax wanting nothing more than to select auto-fire and cut loose with his rifle, spraying plasma projectiles indiscriminately at the horde, yet he knew better than to give into that urge.

Early in the war with the Garm, most soldiers had done just that, and while it made for a brilliant display of carnage and firepower, the marine would be left with an empty weapon and yet more enemies upon him. It was better to lean on one's training and maintain fire discipline, selecting individual targets for confirmed elimination, and only then moving to the next opponent.

The Garm, like the cockroaches of Earth, were notorious for persisting in battle despite being inflicted with grievous wounds. The only Garm you could ignore was a dead Garm. And sometimes not even then.

The marine used his iron sights to draw a bead on a shrieker and squeezed the trigger. The weapon bucked in his hands and spat a super-heated bolt of plasma at the shrieker.

The bolt, despite its tremendously high temperature, held just enough of its solid form to impact against the chiton of the beast. The plasma burned its way through the body armor and as it burrowed into the creature's flesh, it melted into a thick super-heated liquid that rapidly spread throughout the shrieker's body. The shrieker exploded in midair as all the fluids and gases inside it expanded because of the plasma, raining smoldering pieces of flesh down upon the trench floor.

Ajax did not pause to revel in his first kill of the day, and instead selected his next target and fired. His aim was true, and another shrieker died in flight.

The pulse rifles had been designed specifically for combat against the Garm swarms and their deadly efficiency was apparent. Traditional projectile weapons, propelled by ignited powder, might have been much more effective at long ranges, but they were a heavy drain on the already strained human military complex. The sheer scale of the conflict against the swarm made it impossible to keep up with production, so a compact and robust plasma-pulse rifle had been created. What it lost in range it made up for in power, not to mention the fact that ammunition could be made from carbon base blocks, so nearly any substance could be forged into ammunition to feed the Einherjar war machine.

The shriekers reached their firing range and unleashed streaks of viscous fluid from the wicked muzzles of their stubby weapons.

Ajax shouted as he caught sight of a shrieker firing upon a marine several meters from his position.

Yao was a rifle and had been rushing along the bottom of the trench, presumably to help another marine who seemed to have been hit by one of the spore globules. Yao was pumping plasma rounds into two wounded shriekers that had landed near his fallen comrade. The shrieker from above missed the first time, and a jet of foul liquid cut a rivulet through the reinforced wall of the trench behind Yao. The rifle took notice and both he and Ajax drilled the shrieker with bolts.

"On your left!" shouted Rama, and Ajax turned to fire just in time, as several shriekers were swooping down to make a strafing run of the entire parallel.

"I see them," came the gravelly voice of Boone as he too swung left. He used his thumb to select the shortest fuse mod on his launcher before lending his fire to the other marines.

Ajax squeezed the trigger and marveled at the devastating maneuver the shriekers were attempting. While most of the Garm fliers were coming over the trench and diving directly down to attack the marines, a clutch of them had flown in a wide arc that allowed them to strafe the trench lengthwise.

Ajax saw a marine's melting corpse falling backwards off a firing step. The man had been slain from behind without even realizing the attack was coming.

The marine was only one man, but Hydra Company would feel the sting of his loss, as they would the others who had already died and the many more who were yet to do so on this grim evening.

For the swarm, however, life was cheap. As individuals, Garm casualties were just bodies to be recycled. The embodiment of the end justifying the means.

Ajax and Rama harassed the clutch, each of them firing bolts as fast as they could while maintaining a careful aim, as they were firing back down the trench in the direction of their comrades.

The light of the disrupted flare salvo had begun to die down, so when Boone cut loose with his launcher, the trench lit up brilliantly. The grenadier had selected a fuse mod that effectively turned his incendiary rounds into air-bursts. As he pumped shot after shot at the clutch, they exploded among the creatures to create a hurricane of shrapnel that wiped them out.

Yao screamed wetly.

Ajax whipped his head and rifle around to see that the fallen marine Yao had attempted to assist was now on his feet attacking Yao.

Each marine had their name etched into the breastplate of their combat armor, though the ichor of the spores had obscured the man's name. Ajax realized he must have either been struck by one of the spore artillery rounds or been standing nearby when one impacted. Nearly half of the marine's body was covered in the slimy spore mass.

From this distance Ajax couldn't see how the spores had breached the marine's armor or respirator but they clearly had.

The spores had transformed the unknown marine into the murderous psychopath commonly referred to as a ragman.

As Yao struggled against the babbling marine, a man who only moments before had been his comrade, his assailant managed to stab him in the throat with the titanium spike they all carried for close quarters fighting.

"Meat!" howled the ragman, trying to pull the spike from the wound in Yao's throat. The fierce marine held the ragman's wrist in place, causing the two of them to fall to the ground at the bottom of the trench.

Ajax did not hesitate and leapt from the firestep. His boots sank into the mud that had been created by the blood and spores that had been pouring from bodies and falling from the sky. The ragman looked up from his struggle and roared at Ajax as the marine strode toward the pair. Ajax raised his rifle and put a bolt through the armored visor of the marine's helmet.

The plasma rifles had been designed for use against the Garm's natural body armor, while the marine standard issue combat armor had been designed to protect them from the Garm's own weaponry. The hardened ceramic armor of the marine's visor shattered from the impact of the bolt, though the ragman within was shielded from the heat behind the plexi-glass faceplate underneath the visor.

"Meat!" cackled the ragman in a sickeningly jovial voice as he charged Ajax, who then began firing rapidly, each bolt tearing away another piece of the ragman's hardened armor and pushing him back, yet failing to stop him.

Suddenly, the ragman howled in pain as Yao appeared behind him, having risen to one knee so that he could drive the point of his own trench spike deep between the ragman's shoulder blades.

The attack gave Ajax a critical moment to aim his weapon at one of the exposed parts of the ragman's body glove, where the armor had been blasted off. Now that there was no armor to save him the ragman's body exploded just as messily and swiftly as the shriekers when Ajax's bolt bit into him. Yao was thrown back to the ground by the wet explosion. He did not rise again, his life finally spent.

Ajax looked down as his fallen comrades for a moment, watching with transfixed curiosity as the polished steel torc around Yao's neck crackled with an electrical discharge. It was by this discharge that he knew Yao had expired and it made Ajax involuntarily reach up to touch his own torc, suddenly keenly aware of its tightness around the base of his neck.

He was suddenly knocked to the ground as a body smashed into him. He thrashed in the mud beneath its weight until he was out from under it.

A shrieker lay near him, half its body gone and its various entrails spilling out across the churning mud. The sight of it drew Ajax back into the battle at hand, and he raised his rifle to the sky once more.

There were few shriekers left now, only dozens streaking through the darkness where scant minutes before there had been hundreds. The unique chum- chum sound of the quad-barrel anti-air battery filled his ears and Ajax realized he'd been hearing it for a while now. The crew of the gun battery must have successfully eliminated the ragmen that had been transformed in their area by the ridgeback artillery spores.

Watch Tower was back in the fight and was in the process of clearing the skies with extreme prejudice. It was chilling to consider that had the spore barrage eliminated the battery with a combination of impact casualties and ragmen transformations, a portion of the shrieker swarm would likely have been able to pass over Hydra Company and assault the rest of the Einherjar forces with deadly effect. There wouldn't have been enough of them to turn the tide on their own, but perhaps the enemy had something else in store, a diversion within a diversion.

Ajax shuddered at the prospect and did his best to take his mind off such musings as they were too terrible to consider.

Bodies continued to fall from the sky over Trench 16 as Ajax made his way back to the firing step. He saw up and down the parallel that while the marines had indeed suffered casualties from the shrieker swarm, they were recovering from the assault and reforming the defensive perimeter.

Ajax knew that had Watch Tower not gotten the battery into the fight there would be many more dead marines in the trench, possibly most of Hydra Company, as without the protection of the big gun their defenses were vulnerable to air assault.

"They're learning, the bastards," grumbled Boone as Ajax joined the grenadier and Rama once more on the firing step. "That move to strafe the parallel, pretty advanced trench warfare tactic for a bunch of space bugs."

"They adapt," intoned Ajax, almost absent-mindedly as he ejected his spent carbon magazine and slid another into place.

"I hate that saying," spat Boone, "Kinda gives them power, ya know."

"Respect your enemy, that's all it means," responded Rama as he watched the last of the shriekers plummet to its death. "They'll keep attacking until the whole swarm is dead, but just like us they learn from those deaths, and they come at us in a new way. Honestly, we should have expected something like that. Target our battery, smash the trench from the sky before moving on to flank our brothers. There would be hardly any of us left here to fight when the rippers and the gorehounds come."

"A forward observer, who knows our weapons? Seriously, Rama, I don't want to think about that. I just wanna kill things," argued Boone, his worsening demeanor reminding Ajax that the grenadier had been displaying a growing number of warning signs since their arrival on Heorot.

"Second wave!" said the resonating voice of the Watchman, snapping all the marines to attention again. "Flares up!"

"Hold that thought, Boone, I think someone is knocking on the door," said Rama as he ignited another flare and fired it into the darkness above.

This time the dozens of flares fired from the trench rose without incident and reached their apex high above the defense perimeter. Once they hit max height they began to burn, illuminating the area as they sailed in a slow arc over the battlefield in the direction of where it was supposed that the enemy lines were positioned.

As soon as the light shone down, the oncoming nightmare wave of flesh and claws was revealed. They were legion, many thousands of darkly colored chitonous bodies, slavering jaws, and primed projectile weapons of all kinds.

And they were close.

"Hydra Company, swarm advancing!" sounded the deep voice of the Watchman in the earpiece of every marine in Trench 16 who still drew breath. "Stand and deliver!"

On the trench line, there were two chain-fire gun emplacements, each of them a rotating multi-barreled weapon that fired the same plasma bolts that the rifles did, only with an incredible rate of fire. As with the tanks, it had been a long war, and resources were stretched thin, so that Trench 16 even had two such support weapons was a boon.

From his position, Ajax, could see the hundreds of bolts ripping into the wall of alien flesh that roared towards them. Like most ground swarms, the enemy creatures leading the charge were ripper drones, seemingly mindless monsters with multiple limbs tipped by scything chitin blades. More than any other Garm brood they most resembled the cockroach of Earth, armored and voracious, each one was two meters in length and bipedal. They always charged directly at their enemies and carried no projectile weapons, so they usually died in droves as they pressed towards defended positions.

As expected, the chain-fires were tearing a bloody swathe through the legions of ripper drones illuminated by the flares. As brutal as the massacre was, every marine on the line knew that if any of those creatures reached the trench there would be a grisly price to pay, not to mention the fact that behind the rippers would be other swarms, equally deadly and eager for the slaughter.

Ajax leveled his sights at the oncoming enemy and waited for them to hit the first range marker. Each marine trained endlessly to be able to judge distances with the naked eye, an especially useful skill when fighting on various worlds with such varied atmospheric conditions. The war with the Garm had been a brutal thing indeed, with catastrophic losses on both sides, and yet humanity had all but halted the advance of the extinction fleet in the Vorhold system.

As a common soldier, Ajax was not privy to the full complexities of the vast galactic conflict, though he had gathered over time that humanity's back was against the wall and if the Vorhold system fell there would be precious little to keep the swarms away from Earth.

Vorhold was a long way from here, thought Ajax, as he watched the ripper drones being gunned down, but to the people huddling together in the city behind him this was the only front that mattered.

The bulk of the ripper swarm was willingly slain to exhaust the ammunition of the chain-fires and advance the other Garm formations under the cover of their sacrifice. That was the way of the swarm, each part of it fulfilling a specific role without fear or regard for individual survival.

In the pale light of the flares Ajax saw the next swarm come into range, and his heart pounded in his chest.

They were gorehounds, monstrous creatures roughly the size of a human being, only they were stooped creatures that ran on four hoofed feet. With two other limbs that sickeningly resembled clawed arms they carried projectile weapons. Like the shriekers and all the other Garm they had both reptilian and insectoid qualities, but to Ajax they looked like sub-machine guns on four legs.

Their weapons were extensions of their bodies despite how similar they might look to the weapons carried by the warriors of humanity. It was as if the creature's entire body was designed to allow it to rush an enemy position and then empty the magazine, which happened to be the internal contents of their bodies, into the defenders.

"Gorehounds," sneered Boone as he toggled back the fuse mod of his grenade launcher. "This is what they get for keeping their ammo on the inside."

Boone started squeezing the trigger of his launcher, which made a coughing sound every time an explosive round left the barrel.

Ajax held his fire, not wanting to waste bolts, and watched as the rounds punched into the line of enemy creatures.

While some of the rounds hit into the hoofed feet of the gorehounds, the creature's heavily armored heads and shoulders deflected most of them.

Boone had anticipated as much, however, and as the fuses sparked, the grenades ripped holes in the Garm formations. The explosions and shrapnel of the grenades that had landed just behind the oncoming gorehounds were most effective, since the creatures had little armor on the rest of their bodies. As the explosions tore through them, the living ammunition inside each of the gorehounds was exposed to open air.

As had been discovered the hard way by marines in past engagements, the larval ammunition of the gorehounds were inert until they were exposed to breathable air. Once they were awakened, the larvae were voracious and would chew their way through as much living tissue as they could until they literally burst from overeating.

In the blink of an eye Boone's incendiary assault was made even more devastating as many gorehounds who had only been wounded by the blasts were eaten alive from the inside by their own ammunition.

Other grenadiers had made similar choices with their fuse mods and in an instant the swarm had been dealt a mighty blow.

Ajax lost no more time in selecting a target, and fired a bolt through the chest of a gorehound that died as it exploded into several grisly pieces.

The other marines up and down the line began to fire their own plasma rifles. Everyone knew that while the swarm had suffered heavy casualties, behind those gorehounds were yet more horrific creatures, and once the enemies reached the trench the fight would be on the Garm's terms.

Ajax and Rama maintained a steady stream of fire, each marine working the action of their rifle to vent chamber heat after every tenth shot. As rifles they trained hard to make the operation of the weapon as seamless as possible. Against the swarm there was a risk of overheating the weapon, and after every tenth shot the marines vented the heat to keep the rifle operational.

Ajax knew that every time he vented that was one less bolt he fired downrange, one less enemy slain on the field, but it had to be done to be effective for the length of the engagement. Like the prohibition on full-auto spray that was a natural urge in moments of raw fear, the vent on the tenth shot was a rifle discipline drilled into each marine until it was as natural as breathing.

He did his best not think of the innumerable waves of creatures that awaited behind the ripper drones and gorehounds and forced from his mind the sickening realization that a swarm of this size and complexity was not what Hydra Company had prepared to fight.

The Garm had modified their strategy and the rifles of Hydra Company would not be enough to stem the tide.

Ajax drew in a breath and let it out slowly, re-gaining his composure, his only thought was on shoot, vent, and shoot again. It was only through strict rifle discipline that Trench 16 would hold, and hold it they must.

"Hydra Company tactical retreat to the second parallel! First unit, time now!" shouted the voice of Jarl Mahora, the leader of Hydra Company, second only to the Watchman, through everyone's earpiece, "Second unit hold the line!"

Ajax and Boone both stopped firing as soon as commanded and looked at Rama, who briefly nodded to them before returning to aiming his rifle at the enemy.

Ajax and Boone were part of first unit, while Rama was second unit. Everyone knew after much experience fighting the Garm, that a significant portion of second unit would not survive the retreat. They were more of a rearguard who would buy first unit time to escape and re-position.

Ajax leapt down into the mud of the trench bottom and moved as quickly as he could through the thick soup towards the connecting trench. The second parallel was just as fortified as the first, but even though it occupied a smaller swathe of ground, the marines still had to sprint down roughly eighty meters of trench to reach it.

There were only three connecting trenches, spaced evenly across the first parallel, so the two marines had a treacherous distance to cover to reach the connection.

Ajax tried to maintain a good speed while struggling against the sucking mud and the carnage the covered the bottom of the trench. What ground wasn't covered in treacherous mud was littered with the broken bodies of shriekers and more than a few marines. As the two marines picked their way down the trench, the men of second unit kept firing into the oncoming waves of Garm.

Ajax was passing near one of the chain-fire emplacement when the gun overheated and suddenly went silent as the action of the weapon slammed into place, a security feature that kept it from exploding.

It was an odd feature, but a useful one. When the chain-fires were first introduced to the battlefield they had a nasty habit of exploding when they overheated. They had been created like the pulse rifles of the infantry, and relied upon individual gunners to manually vent the excess heat caused by firing the weapon.

However, the limits of human control over the instincts of fight or flight was limited, and it had been discovered that in the thick of battle most gunners were incapable of choosing to stop firing if they were in a desperate situation. When facing the scuttling horrors of the Garm, all they could do was keep shooting, so the automatic safety action had to be placed on each weapon. If the gunner did not pause to vent the heat, after a while the gun would just shut down, preserving the weapon.

Ajax could hear the gunners cursing in frustration as they raised their rifles, each knowing that the gun would have to cool for several minutes and by that time this trench would be lost. That was the element about the shut off that Ajax found most strange, yet cruelly effective. If the gun was pushed to such limits that it shut down, one could safely assume that whatever position being defended would be overrun. With the gun shut down it was unlikely to be damaged by the swarm, for it was not organic or operational. If the Einherjar could turn the tide of battle and retake the position, the gun would be waiting for them, cooled off and ready to fire in an instant. One of the many bizarre tactics learned by the Einherjar during this seemingly endless war against the swarm.

Ajax reached the connecting tunnel, with Boone right behind him and they picked up the pace on more solid ground.

The connecting trench had been cut into the loamy soil and then reinforced with flak-boards just like the first parallel, though it had not suffered from the battle with the shrieker swarm. Only a handful of rifles stood guard in the trench, and so there was little to attract the attention of the creatures. The marines raced down the trench and were about halfway to the second parallel when they heard Mahora's voice over the company channel once more.

"Second unit, yield the parallel!" ordered Mahora in the earpiece of each marine, and then followed that with, "Prepare the Blackouts for deployment!"

Ajax and Boone, with a score of other first unit marines, reached the second parallel and immediately began working to prepare its defense.

Only a handful of marines were already in position on the second parallel and as the marines from first unit poured in, the trench line began to bristle with rifles.

Boone slung his empty launcher and drew his sidearm, a pistol equivalent of the pulse rifles carried by the other marines, smaller in bolt caliber but it still packed quite a punch.

Ajax took a few seconds to swap out his carbon mag for a fresh one. While he still had plenty of ammunition left in the first, the next wave of enemies might not give him the chance to switch later.

"Ajax!" said a friendly voice to his right, and as the marine turned he saw his comrade, Sharif, standing on a firestep near the connecting trench, another rifle and a member of the casual circle of friends that all soldiers formed naturally over the course of any war. "Where's Yao?"

"He didn't make it this time," answered Boone over his shoulder as he planted his feet at the edge of the connecting trench, seemingly having made his choice to defend that position, considering that his pistol would not do as well as a rifle on the open ground above. "You seen Hart anywhere?"

"I haven't, but that's kind of the point, right?" answered Sharif before gesturing back towards the anti-air gun battery up the hill, "Some trouble at Watch Tower I think, so the jarl sent him to check it out."

"It did look like Tower got hit pretty hard with the spore barrage," said Ajax as marines from second wave started to make their way down the connecting tunnel.

BLACKOUTS

"*Guns up! Here they come!*" bellowed Jarl Mahora as the large veteran warrior emerged from the press of marines in the trench to take a position near the opening of the connecting tunnel. "Blackouts into position!"

Ajax stepped aside, as did the other marines, with a mixed sense of reverence and fear as the troopers known as 'Blackouts' were led down the trench and to the connecting tunnels by their minders.

Every Einherjar was, for all intents and purposes, the same man he was when he first accepted the torc, the minders were just average marines, but the Blackouts were something else entirely.

Each one had been a marine, but the rigors of this endless war with the Garm had taken a toll on their minds, their very spirits, as much as it had their bodies. Blackouts were marines who had succumbed to what had everyone called 'the black', which was an unquenchable murderous rage that stayed with a marine no matter how many times the torc worked its miracle.

They had to be separated from the other marines, and kept imprisoned until those in command chose to unleash them upon the enemy. The Blackouts wore the same ceramic armor as the other marines, but instead of the dull camo patterns of the standard armor, theirs was painted in matte black, a symbol of their rage.

Two minders restrained the Blackouts by staffs attached to rivets in a collar at the base of their neck, which kept them from being within arm's reach of anyone. The Blackouts possessed such an abiding hatred for the Garm, they would kill or injure any marine that stood between them and the swarm and it was best to keep them well managed until deployment.

Sharif and the others on the firesteps opened fire and Ajax knew that the first parallel was lost. The swarm was already crossing the no man's land between the parallels, which meant that they'd filled the first with countless bodies of Garm and marine. Ajax could see in the murky distance several marines rushing down the connecting trench, the enemy only a few steps behind.

As he watched, a ripper drone got close enough to launch itself into the air with its powerful legs and down onto the back of a fleeing marine. The drone's scythe like appendages sheared off pieces of the ceramic armor while it held the marine to the ground with its other limbs and its very weight. In seconds, the drone had worked its blades through the gaps in the armor and shredded the man within.

Ajax and another marine raised their rifles and blasted the drone to pieces, taking care not to catch the downed marine in the crossfire. Ajax kept firing into the trench, having trouble telling what kind of Garm he was firing upon in the gloom. He paused in his shooting as one of the minders shouldered him aside.

At a nod from Mahora, a third minder placed a heavy-duty automatic plasma pistol in one of the Blackout's hands and a forty-inch titanium blade in the other that looked more like a meat cleaver to Ajax than a proper sword.

The Blackout shook with rage and Ajax could tell that the voice mics inside the helmet had been intentionally deactivated, to spare the other marines on the company channel the insane ramblings of the Blackout, who spoke only of the explicit ways in which they wanted to kill Garm.

The swarm poured through the trench even as the rifles on the firesteps did their best to repel the monsters that attacked them across open ground.

"Deploy Blackouts!" ordered Mahora, giving the signal. The minders who had positioned Blackouts at the opening of each connecting trench released the catch on their charge's collar. "Eight-man counter attack in his wake! Step up marines!"

Ajax steadied himself as the Blackout sprinted into the connecting trench, knowing that by standing at the opening and not ascending the firing step he'd basically volunteered himself for the counter attack. That was the nature of trench warfare against the swarm, the two opposing forces would grind against one another, pushing each other back and forth across the battlefield, until one or the other force was either obliterated or yielded the ground. It was a tedious and mind-numbingly gory way to wage war, and ultimately the only effective method of pushing back against the swarm.

Ajax gritted his teeth and tightened his shoulders as he watched the Blackout collide with the enemy, knowing that any second Mahora was going to launch the counter attack.

The Blackout, whose name had been obscured by the paint on his armor and the madness burning through his mind, hurled himself into battle. He raised his machine pistol and squeeze the trigger, spitting a tempest of bolts into the writhing mass of alien beasts.

The machine pistols used by the Blackouts were single use weapons, holding just enough ammunition to reach peak core temperature before exhausting the magazine. Constructing them in this way, without regard for damage done to the internal components, allowed the Blackouts to fire nearly three times the bolts, without venting, before the weapon was useless.

The Blackout never broke stride, rushing headlong towards the enemy, spraying rounds as he leapt over the smoldering corpses of those already slain.

"Marines on me!" growled Jarl Mahora as he gripped his pulse rifle and started marching into the connecting trench.

Ajax knew that the marines on the firesteps would be doing their best to keep the swarm from reaching the second parallel. Most of those would-be ripper drones and gorehounds, either survivors of the first swarm or more likely a reserve force that followed close on the heels of the initial wave. There might be worse creatures out there, but for a force assaulting a secondary objective like Hydra Company's position, this was about what he expected. Ajax trusted his fellow marines to keep the shots coming and to hold the attention of the enemy to prevent them from flanking the counter attack.

The marine pushed himself to keep pace with Mahora as the jarl followed behind the Blackout's wake of carnage. The Blackout had only been engaged with the enemy for a few seconds, but already he'd mowed through a dozen of the beasts. Ajax caught a glimpse of the former marine dropping his spent machine pistol in favor of his sword. The Blackout spun on his heels and swept the blade around in a wide arc that covered the width of the trench, cleaving two ripper drones into pieces as the precision sharpened blade passed through them.

As the Blackout slashed his way through another drone, Ajax thought that if the warrior had been facing human beings the fear of his bloody display would have driven the enemy into retreat. Sadly, there would never be any such luck against the Garm, for the alien swarm knew no fear and they attacked him without regard for their own survival.

The Blackout reached the opening of the connecting trench and there his rampage was cut short. A gorehound had taken up position at the mouth of the connecting trench. The creature's weapon appendage roared, spewing out a great gout of wriggling larva that swept the Blackout off his feet.

In the blink of an eye, the larvae that had not splattered against the ceramic armor of the former marine struck at the few gaps in the joints of his armor and chewed their way into the man's body.

Each of the creatures was born exclusively to feed and though they were only perhaps a centimeter long the creatures ate their way through flesh as fast as any bullet could rend. As they chewed, their bodies bloated with the feast until they burst apart, creating wet secondary explosions inside the Blackout's already ravaged body.

Mahora did not allow the ambush to go unanswered and pounded a bolt through the gorehound's neck, swiftly decapitating it as the plasma burned through it. Ajax and the rest of the marines emerged from the connecting trench to form a tight wedge of rifles that started firing upon the gorehounds that stubbornly remained in the trench.

Ajax could read the fate of second unit in an instant, knowing that most of them had sold their lives dearly on the line before Mahora ever called for full retreat. This sacrifice was by design of course, as the eventual retreat of the marines pulled the swarm into the trenches themselves, their raw hunger driving the monsters to take the most direct path towards their prey. With the ripper drones and gorehounds bottled up in the connecting trench, they were set for slaughter by the Blackout and the resulting counter attack had a chance of retaking the trench.

"*WarGarm!*" shouted a marine and Ajax turned around just in time to catch a glimpse of the creature before being knocked aside by Mahora.

The WarGarm were the elite warriors of the swarm, nightmare amalgamations of the lesser broods that stood easily three meters in height. The creatures were covered in armor like that of the gorehounds, sported scythe appendages like the ripper drones, and carried ferocious projectile weapons in their awful hands. Where the other broods fought in groups, the WarGarm stalked the battlefields alone, fighting to support the greater actions of their more numerous kin.

The monster's weapon emitted a high pitched keening noise and coughed up several twelve inch projectiles that had always reminded Ajax of the quills belonging to the porcupines of Earth.

The marine who had first seen the creature was now riddled with spines and had fallen to the ground, jackknifing with spasms that were likely the result of the horrific toxins contained within the already deadly projectiles. Mahora took two in the side, but they appeared to be embedded in his armor and did not seem to have pierced his body glove to sink into his flesh, though the ceramic was cracked and would need replacing.

Boone shouted and started firing his pistol, but the creature's body armor was sufficiently stout to deflect the shots. The WarGarm exchanged fire with Boone and another marine who had lent his pulse rifle to the fight, the latter managing to blow apart one of the WarGarm's scythe appendages before he was pierced with four spines and splashed down into the mud.

From where he'd landed after Mahora's shove, Ajax could see that the other marines were busily shooting it out with several gorehounds on the other end of the trench, one of the marines already writhing in the mud as he was consumed by the larva rounds.

Mahora pushed himself off Ajax and raised his rifle to fire from a crouched position. His bolt rounds spanked off the WarGarm's armor but he managed to spoil its aim. A line of spines sunk into the trench wall above Boone, a salvo that would surely have killed him.

"Ajax, get that chain-fire online and turn it back on the second parallel!" snapped the jarl as he and Boone, who had taken up his fallen comrade's rifle, concentrated their fire on the WarGarm, driving the beast into the far wall of the trench and destroying its weapon.

Ajax did his best to ignore the violence around him as he climbed the short ladder leading up to the gun emplacement. When he reached the top rung, he saw the mangled corpse of the gunner spread across the deck. Once he stood on the emplacement he had to kick over the charred remains of a ripper drone so that he could swivel the weapon back towards the second parallel. The flares that had illuminated no man's land were sinking to the ground, though in their dying light and the partial illumination of a fresh batch of flares shot from the second parallel, Ajax could see the mess that had been made of the swarm.

The ground in front of the first parallel was choked with corpses. On top of them writhed the broken bodies of the many gorehounds and ripper drones that had been wounded, each one driven to carry on despite the heinous damage they'd been dealt.

Mercifully, the strength of the swarm seemed to have been spent on seizing the first parallel and the aborted assault on the second parallel, as no more enemies charged out of the darkness to reinforce the beleaguered Garm that clung to their briefly won territory.

Ajax thumbed the ignition and the chain-fire snarled to life as the marine heaved the gun around on the swivel so that he could bring it to bear on the second parallel.

Ajax took in the sight of the battleground. While there were far fewer rifles defending the second parallel and no chain-fires, the marines were keeping up a steady rate of disciplined shooting that had so far managed to keep the swarm from overrunning the trench.

Mortars would have been an effective way of defending Trench 16, but prolonged galactic warfare and the unique complications of combat against the swarm had made mortars ineffective, not to mention the Garm's unique ability to shrug off concussive damage that would otherwise kill most organisms.

Ajax peered through the target finder and chambered the first of two remaining ammo drums. It made sense, he thought, sighting in on a clutch of gorehounds who were exchanging fire with a few rifles on the edges of the illumination offered by the flares, that the marines would find that the best way to fight the Garm was to burn them.

Ajax squeezed the trigger and the chain-fire belched out dozens of bolt rounds that quickly reduced half of the gorehounds to quivering lumps of smoldering alien flesh. The remaining gorehounds were thrown into confusion by the crossfire, allowing the rifles on the second parallel to exploit the moment and wipe them out with concentrated fire.

Ajax swept the barrel of the chain-fire across no man's land, taking care not to fire into the connecting trench, and blasted at clusters of Garm that were still out in the open. Though it had cost them lives, thought Ajax as he drilled another group of ripper drones, it was good that the War-Garm had made an appearance.

The Einherjar had learned early in the war that the swarm always followed the biggest and the baddest bug in the area and that usually meant the WarGarm. By having Mahora and the others tangling with it down in the trench and the counter attack in general, the swarm now caught in no man's land was in a state of disarray. Some were far enough into the fray they continued to assault the second parallel, while others fought in the trench against the counter attack. Still more seemed to be rushing towards the area where the WarGarm struggled for its very life.

Ajax couldn't see the beast, but he could hear its pained bleating over the sound of gunfire, and as expected, he was met with groups of Garm attempting to reach it.

He was being as selective as he could with the chain-fire, doing his best to vent the heat, but as he kept peppering the exposed enemy, Ajax began to wonder why he hadn't heard anything from the Watchman since the call for flares had gone out. Then he caught sight of Hart in his target finder. It was all he could do to release the trigger when the scout sniper entered his field of fire.

Ajax blinked. He'd swear a long, dark shape had slithered into the gloom and vanished outside the half-light of the flares, then he lost sight of Hart as well.

"Hydra Company, leave rearguard in position and advance on the first parallel!" boomed Jarl Mahora from somewhere down in the trench below. Ajax saw through his target finder as dozens of marines emerged from their firesteps and started marching across no man's land.

Ajax only dared to fire upon individual Garm for a few more moments, before abandoning the chain-fire in favor of his rifle. It would not do to cause any friendly fire incidents and the chain-fire had done its job beautifully. Now it was on individual rifles to engage the enemy and secure the trench.

Without the target finder, Ajax couldn't see the advancing marines, though he knew from his own training and experience that they were marching in a straight line, like an execution squad or the military formations of ancient times. They would sweep across no man's land, herding the Garm that remained, finishing off the wounded, and then re-taking the trench. Ajax could do little from where he was, and determined that he was needed back in the trench.

The marine leapt off the gun emplacement and moved across the lip of the trench on the Garm side. He had his back to the enemy's frontline, however distant, but did his best not to be afraid of that nagging truth. From his vantage point Ajax saw that the jarl and his counter attack had been able to finish off the War-Garm, turning its body into smoldering pulp and bits of shattered armor. The marine snapped the rifle to his shoulder and put two bolt rounds into a gorehound he saw rising from beneath a pile of Garm and marine corpses, then continued his march across the length of the trench.

The swarm was a single-minded thing, and once it launched an attack all the creatures would press onwards until the very last one died or victory was achieved. While this made for terrifying battles at the outset, if the marines could hold out long enough to break the strength of the swarm against their ramparts, much of the battle would continue as it was now. This terrifying blitzkrieg of a battle had transformed into a seek and destroy mission, as the once mighty Garm swarm had been reduced to small clutches of beasts or individual monsters that yet stalked the field in search of prey.

Mahora, Boone, and another marine moved along the bottom of the trench while Ajax covered them from the top. They encountered a few ripper drones, most of them wounded, and one more gorehound before marines from the second parallel joined them in the hunt. Still nothing from the Watchman, noted Ajax as he and a marine on top of the other side of the trench combined their fire to slay a gorehound attempting to take aim at the marines advancing from below. It was then that Ajax heard a single shot ring out, a different report than that made by the pulse rifles or sickening Garm weapons. It was a kinetic weapon, large caliber, with lots of explosive power behind it.

Hart.

Ajax turned around and faced the darkness of no man's land, opening his eyes as wide as he could to take in some details of the gloom. He tried to see past the wounded Garm, as if staring into the darkness would give him some scrap of intel.

There.

A second shot sounded and this time he saw the muzzle flash of what he knew had to be Hart's special issue sniper rifle. Nobody but the scout snipers carried weapons that fired actual bullets, as they were too resource intensive for the protracted war against the alien invaders.

Ajax turned around to look behind him and saw that the rest of the marines had moved on with securing the trench. He was alone on this side of the trench, with naught but corpses and wounded Garm as company.

Somewhere out there in the darkness Hart was hunting something and as much as his instincts screamed at him not to go, Ajax began moving towards where he'd seen the muzzle flash.

The marine gingerly picked his way across the corpse-littered ground, careful to stay well away from the few wounded Garm that thrashed in futility as he pressed into no man's land. Soon the flares were in the distance and he could only see a few feet in front of him.

A strange sound came from his left, something akin to what he imagined two wet bones scraping against each other might make, and he swept his rifle around to meet it. Nothing moved, only dead Garm laying still, and yet again he heard the sound.

Ajax turned, his eyes catching a glimpse of a serpentine tail comprised of many sections of interlocking chitin, leading up to the thick torso of a creature that had to be equal to the size of a WarGarm. It was covered in spiny appendages and had strange frills jutting up from its back. Its face, however, shared the same reptilian and yet, insectoid features of the other Garm.

"The forward observer," whispered Ajax as he raised his weapon to his shoulder and placed his finger on the trigger.

What kept him from firing wasn't so much the creature's wicked maw of tendrils and hinged pincers, but the dull reflection of the flares against its matte black eyes that memorized him.

Ajax barely noticed when the meter-long blade of razor-sharp chitin slid into his abdomen and up through his heart.

The entire galaxy had become those awful eyes.

In the background of his fading consciousness Ajax was dimly aware of the sharp crack of a familiar sniper rifle and then all was darkness.

THE CHOSEN SLAIN

Lightning surged through the darkness.

Synapses fired anew. Neurons awakened once more. Organs began to function again. The body of a man crackled with energy, and the mind of a marine achieved consciousness.

Ajax opened his eyes and inhaled deeply.

He was instantly aware of the torc around his neck, and no sooner had he noticed it than another bolt of lightning hammered through his body.

The data recorded on the torc comprised the whole of his memories, mapped and coded by the miracles of science that had allowed humanity to thrive and survive in this harsh universe. Chemicals in the marine's brain reacted to the coded instructions, and as the man's awareness was engulfed by the electric tempest his memories were returned to him.

Ajax roared in pain and exultation as he was simultaneously reborn and resurrected.

In the storm, he found himself standing on a barren mountainside of scrabble stone and ash. In the burning yellow sky, great lumbering beasts drifted on the winds, held up by gargantuan gas bladders and dragging incredibly long tentacles behind them. The tentacles went all the way to the ground, and from there burst into many more smaller tendrils, effectively sweeping across the land. He could see tiny bits of vegetation and organic matter caught in the tendrils and pulled up the network into the beasts.

In the distance, there was a city, its skyline somehow familiar to Ajax, though it had been so ruined by time and artillery that he could not place it. The air stank of organic discharge and static electricity, and the marine's eyes teared up at the potency of it.

The marine spun on his heels, his fists clenched for violence, and saw a beautiful woman not a few steps from him. He recognized her,

35

impossibly, as his wife, Rowan, a woman long dead at the hands of the Garm invasion.

He did not move as she gingerly stepped towards him, painfully aware of the swell of her bosom and the sway of her hips as she moved, dressed as she was in garb that made him think of the myths upon which the Einherjar military was based. As in the stories of old she tipped a stein of mead to his lips, and he drank deeply of the honeyed liquid as if his thirst was bottomless. His belly rumbled and the woman pressed a sizzling strip of meat in his mouth. It wasn't the flavorless molded protein of the barracks mess hall, but actual flesh that tasted as if it had been roasted over an open fire. She pressed herself against him suggestively, as if she knew how terribly lonely a man could become on such an endless battlefield as his, and she smiled as she gently guided him to the ground.

Surely, the Valkyrie were just part of a story, the myth from one of Earth's ancient cultures, he thought to himself as her lips touched his and she guided his over her body as she moved on top of him. As they moved together he realized that his wounds were healed, his guts no longer torn and his heart absent the vile blade. Valhalla is just a story, he insisted to himself silently, before the woman lowered herself onto him, and then he thought of no more beyond the exertion of their embrace.

Something moved behind Rowan and the sound of bone grating against bone sent adrenaline coursing through the marine's body. He recognized the sound, and upon hearing it, the memories of his fight in the trench came flooding back to him. Ajax looked back at the woman just as a chitin blade sprouted from her chest, showering him in her bright blood as her body was yanked off him.

Ajax wiped the blood from his face and scrambled to reach his feet. He could hear the beast slithering over the loose stones, though he could not see it. The marine looked about him for a weapon, but found little save a large sharp rock, which he decided would have to do. Ajax held his weapon aloft and moved in a slow circle, following the sound of the creature as it stalked him. He held his vigil, moving in circle after circle, until he began to question if he'd even seen it or heard it at all.

Again, the lightning moved through him and his consciousness was shaken.

THE BODY FORGE

His eyes were sore, and he had a headache, but when he opened his eyes and looked around he saw that he was on a recovery table, presumably aboard the warship Bright Lance. Standing around the low surface were three physician engineers, one of them Ajax recognized as Idris, the chief attendant. He was still restrained on the table, which was a standard procedure after his unconscious form had been removed from the body forge.

Ajax did not resist his bonds, as it was protocol to dock each marine for a short time once emerging from the forge. Not everyone came back peacefully, and sometimes it took a few minutes, sometimes even hours, for someone to sync with the torc. Ajax knew from personal experience that during those first few minutes of life after the forge, one's sense of reality could be rather fluid. Considering the horrors of war that the Einherjar regularly witnessed, it was prudent to restrain them until normalcy could be achieved.

"Welcome back, marine, you are safely aboard the Lance," said Idris as he reached out to touch the marine's shoulder with a reassuring hand. "Please remain at ease while we finish our diagnostic, we must ensure that your expiration was not so traumatic that the body manifests any residual injuries. Your file indicates that this is not likely, but we must be sure, mustn't we?"

"Marine at ease, sir," said Ajax, keeping with protocol even though his mind raced with what he'd seen. Such a potent vision, or hallucination, or whatever it was had never been something he experienced after emerging from the forge. He found it disturbing, as it was known that resurrection dreams were often an early indicator of a marine's eventual Blackout. Such dreams were not always milestones, as plenty of marines had the dreams but had yet to Blackout, though it was well known that everyone who achieved full Blackout suffered the most vivid such dreams.

"All vitals are good, the torc upload is green, but you seemed to suffer a manner of seizure just after you came online," said Idris as he finished his work and then set about gently releasing the restraints on the table.

"While the resurrection dreams are acceptably commonplace, I'd like to schedule a follow up exam in a few weeks just to make sure we didn't overlook something," Idris continued as he offered a helping hand so that Ajax could return to his feet for the first time in this body, "Presuming of course that you survive that long."

"Copy, sir," nodded Ajax as the other two attendants helped him into a standard issue body glove, the movement helping the marine to get his physical bearings and clear his head of cobwebs before he turned to ask, "Did we win?"

"Victory against the Garm is always a relative affair is it not?" said Idris with a grim smile as he gestured to the bustling forge infirmary. "From a tactical perspective, we held the line against the swarm, Heorot remains unmolested, so you are to be congratulated on a job well done, even if it cost us many thousands of lives. With regards to how this setback affects the overall stratagems of the extinction fleet and the army of the All-Father? Who but Odin can know such things?"

Ajax nodded and turned to leave the infirmary, knowing that he was expected to attend a company debriefing with Jarl Mahora.

Each jarl was to gather intelligence from the accounts of their attending company and push the report up to the Watchman, a marine commander who was the master of Einherjar ground forces deployed from Bright Lance. From there he would judge the actions of each marine and their jarl, take what intelligence he could, and use it to add to the overall knowledge of the Garm, adapting any strategies or tactics needed to make the Einherjar a more effective fighting force. It had been considered an honor that Hydra Company was given the task of defending the gun battery that the Watchman had chosen to use as his Tower for that particular engagement.

The marine knew his way from the forge to the hangar bay, knowing that troop shuttles would be making regular departures for the planet's surface. With so many casualties there would be a constant flow of freshly forged marines making their way back to their units in Heorot.

Ajax had made this journey from the body forge seventeen times since joining the ranks of the Einherjar. Most of the marines in his shuttle were members of other companies, though he did see Rama strapped in near the front of the shuttle. The men did not speak as they launched from the bay of the warship and made planetfall, each was busy getting reacquainted with his body and his mind. They had all done this many times, though even experienced clone soldiers had a certain amount of existential work to do before he was fully prepared to return to battle.

HEOROT THE CURSED

Once back on the surface, Ajax reported to his company's basecamp, which had been set up in what appeared to be an equipment warehouse in Heorot that had been converted to suit military purposes. The Hydra Company debriefing went as Ajax expected, with a tally of shots fired, accuracy reports, casualty lists, tactical evaluations, and a respectful welcome for the resurrected.

It had become routine, this dance of death, forging, debriefing, and the swift return to duty. However, his experiences on this most recent battlefield, his resulting death, and the vividly engaging resurrection dream that had been accompanied by a seizure, where not at all routine. Nor was the personal summons he received from Jarl Mahora after the debriefing, since most marines had been ordered either to rest and refit or return to Trench 16 for waste disposal and picket duty.

Ajax entered through the sliding metal door that led to the former warehouse manager's office and was taken aback by the sight that awaited him in the chamber. Jarl Mahora stood at attention with his back to the far wall of the small chamber, in the chair where the jarl usually sat was someone else entirely.

A marine was perched on the edge of the chair, dressed in patchwork armor and camo netting that marked him as a skald, the recon and intelligence commandos from Taskforce Loki. Common grunts such as Ajax, rarely saw them, at least up close, as they were usually deployed on one sort of special mission or the other. Ajax wasn't even aware that the warship Bright Lance had been assigned a skald. The man's helmet was in place despite being in the well-protected fortress ship, but as Ajax took his seat, after a moment's pause, the warrior removed it.

"Marine Ajax, you have the honor of being in the presence of Skald Thatcher," said Mahora with some consternation, giving Ajax the distinct impression that he was not pleased to have had his command

41

somewhat usurped. "He and a cadre of operatives arrived during the nightcycle aboard the scout ship Crimson Shard, sent by the All-Father to assist us in the defense of Heorot."

"Anything we discuss here must be in the strictest confidence," said Thatcher as he leaned forward to steeple his hands and set his armored elbows on the table. "I know how it is out there on the line, in the trenches. Men talk, they are overheard, and knowledge spreads. This we cannot have."

"Sirs, forgive me," stumbled Ajax, their request throwing him into a state of confusion even as he struggled to maintain composure in the presence of such a legendary operative as Skald Thatcher, who had accounted for some of the most daring victories in the long war against the Garm. "The Einherjar have no secrets, so that no man can be above his brother, surely I cannot break that code."

"I told you he was staunch," snorted Jarl Mahora, his eyes blazing with a fierce pride in the marine's unwillingness to break with code, even when asked by such as the skald. "Seventeen trips to the forge and not a dent in the armor."

"That is a relief, I suppose, every warrior fights with the tools for which he is most suited, even if it does present us with a unique difficulty," said Thatcher as he closed his eyes and took a deep breath before looking across the table at Ajax, taking his time in the silence until finally saying, "Our strength is in our unflinching commitment to the cause, and yet we must find ways in which to be flexible in the execution of our duties. The enemy is rather cunning, Ajax, more so than any grunt can imagine. We skald live and breathe both stories and secrets, it is what we do."

"This game of predator/prey that you play with the enemy, we have no taste for," said Mahora, who looked from Ajax to Thatcher, giving the freshly forged marine the impression that Mahora and the skald had been arguing the matter for some time before he entered the room,

"We build walls, dig ditches, set barricades, and we defend them. We watch the gates."

"And yet the enemy games with you regardless," snapped Thatcher, and Ajax found himself concerned for Jarl Mahora, who, while being the top man in Hydra Company, was but a jarl, while this skald had a direct line with Command. "If they can't break your walls down, they will dig them out from under you, and unless you accept that this war has transformed, we will fail."

"Transformed?" asked Ajax, able to stay silent no longer, as he had guessed that he wasn't the first marine this pair had debriefed, not to mention Jarl Mahora's personal experience, so they likely knew about the differences in tactics displayed by the swarm encountered by Hydra Company.

"Heorot has no symmetric tactical significance, little organic material to justify an invasion, and yet here we are knee-deep in corpses," offered Thatcher as he returned his full attention to the marine. "It is my mission to determine why the Garm have come to devour this modest outpost, and why a new beast stalks us here, in this lonely place, and not on battlefields of greater merit."

"You've already debriefed Hart, then I take it," surmised Ajax, as his blood turned cold at the thought of the serpentine creature he'd encountered both on the battlefield and in his resurrection dream. "You know about the forward observer."

"Indeed," smiled Thatcher, a facial expression that Ajax thought terribly inappropriate for the situation. "Hart had more to tell us concerning the beast on the battlefield. I have been informed that you displayed not only the elevated brainwaves indicative of resurrection dreams, but you suffered a minor seizure in the process. Though Idirs insists there is no discernably lasting damage, I am curious to hear of the details."

"They're just hallucinations, sir, caused by the trauma of so many memories being re-coded into a fresh brain," countered Ajax, uncomfortable sharing the explicit intimacies of his dream, especially considering how much it seemed to confirm to the old Norse myths, which struck Ajax as awfully silly in this modern age. "Just the mind re-ordering itself."

"He knows the science, marine," barked Mahora, "Spit it out."

"Start with the first flare and walk us through it," commanded Thatcher as he activated the recorder on his wrist tablet. "I am especially concerned with moments during the engagement when you felt as if you were acting in a way that you found surprising, or if others were displaying inconsistent behaviors."

Ajax took a deep breath and began to speak. It was easy for him to recount his actions in the defense of Trench 16, as such things had become all too routine for the battle-hardened marine. His tone changed when it came time to discuss the creature that had slain him, and the resulting resurrection dreams he'd suffered afterwards.

"You have encountered something new, Ajax, a creature and swarm tactics that we have not yet faced, and it troubles me," said the skald after Ajax was finally able to finish his report, struggling to recall every horrible detail of the beast. "What troubles me more is the resurrection dream, and the possibility that your very consciousness has been compromised."

"Compromised?" breathed Ajax, taken aback at the possibility that his mind was not his own.

"The official stance is that it's just a soldier's mind sorting it all out. No evidence has been presented to the contrary, and we've been at this for a long time," said Mahora, his arms folded across his chest as he leaned against the far wall. "What the skald suggests is that the enemy may have found a way to take a peek at the sorting. That about the long and short of it sir?"

"Close enough for grunts," nodded Thatcher with a faint smile, which melted away as he returned his gaze to Ajax. "You and your comrade were the only marines in the field who actually laid their eyes upon this elusive new creature, despite the dozens of confirmed kills inside Watch Tower, including the Watchman himself. Hart survived his encounter, having driven it away moments after the beast had fatally impaled you. Can you see where I'm going with this?"

"I am the only marine to both see the creature and to have died," answered the marine, the knot in his belly tightening as a feral sort of fear began to take hold.

"The 'forward observer' as you call it, infiltrated our perimeter, either before the spore bombardment or just after. Once inside it sought out the Watchman, slaying any marine that happened to be in the way, with absolute stealth," said Thatcher as he produced a datapad and slid it across the table to Ajax, who saw that it was a series of photos depicting the messy remains of the Watchman. "Whereas the other marines were killed in a similar manner as you were, the Watchman appears to have been held in place as his helmet was destroyed, his skull opened, and his brains vacuumed away."

"What does he say of the creature?" asked Ajax, a knot of fear beginning to form in his guts, "Or has he not yet emerged from the body forge?"

"Now we have come upon the meat of the subject, the prime reason that I require your silence on the specifics," said Thatcher, reaching across the table and scrolling through the photos until he came upon a particularly grisly one of the Watchman's empty skull. "At first, command could not fathom why an enemy combatant would consume only the brain of a victim, as we all know that the ripper drones are somewhat voracious battlefield eaters, and even some of the gorehound have been observed partaking of the flesh of the fallen immediately after an engagement. As you know, combat feeding is part of their standard behavior, to replace the massive amounts of energy they expend during battle.

Thatcher joined Ajax in scrutinizing the photo. "This was a highly selective feeding, quite uncharacteristic, and to our knowledge, the first of its kind. This war has been waged across the stars of our galaxy for many years, and in that time, we have adapted our weapons and tactics to face the specific threat that the swarm poses. It has been a dance between humanity and the enemy, as much a game of move and countermove as it is an arms race to develop the most effective ways of killing each other."

"The Garm adapt," growled Mahora, looking away from the tablet in disgust. "Marines overcome."

"That has indeed been the case so far. The gorehounds evolved all of that barding armor after we introduced the pulse rifle, and the ridgebacks began firing solid ordinance once we began using the rebreathers. Our most important advance has been in the cloning technology that yielded men like us, the Einherjar, giving us the ability to mimic their breeding rates and keep our ranks refreshed. We are denying them a victory by attrition, which by all accounts seemed to have been their overarching strategy. It has all been very symmetrical, in the grand scheme of things," discussed the skald before sitting back in his chair, suddenly looking haggard, as if even the thought of his next statement fatigued him.

"This selective feeding by a new Garm organism represents the first time that the swarm has evolved rather than adapted," he began. "We believe that the creature was responsible for the deaths of our recon scouts, and was sent with a specific mission to harvest the Watchman. We must assume that with that level of selective targeting the purpose must have been to gather intelligence."

"Official briefings state that Garm aren't intelligent, more like a complex hive executing pre-programmed chemical commands that mimic intelligence, like ants or bees back on Earth," argued Ajax incredulously, even though he had a feeling that Thatcher would correct him for regurgitating official doctrine. "An operation like that would take, I don't know, something like abstract thought, the capacity to make value judgements in the selection of prey."

"Which is why we cannot allow this assassination to go unanswered," replied Thatcher. "The enemy assaulted our defenses, knowing to target the anti-air battery with spore fire to protect an initial shrieker swarm. They didn't attack to seize ground or even consume our forces, those were secondary objectives. That was made clear by the timestamp on the Watchman's torc, as the swarm lost its momentum the moment he was terminated, and as you know we were able to wipe them out with relative ease once they stalled in their advance."

"In the absence of the Watchman, command of our forces has gone to Captain Yusef of the Bright Lance, and at his request the All-Father has sent us Skald Thatcher," growled Mahora. "He was the nearest operative in the field, so he and his squad have been re-assigned to Heorot."

"The absence of the Watchman?" asked Ajax, confused at how both the skald and the jarl continued to speak of the commander in the past tense.

"Your commander has not been questioned yet because he died of an uncontrollable seizure moments after resurrection. When Idris brought him back he died the same way once more, the same has been the case for three of the recon scouts," answered Thatcher, his voice grim as he took the datapad back from Ajax and returned it to his pack.

"Whatever the beast did to them seems to have interfered, perhaps permanently, with the mind's ability to accept rebirth," Thatcher continued. "The fact that you suffered a similar, if non-fatal, seizure, and that you both were the only marines to witness the creature, is most curious, and begs for keen observation of your actions during the continued defense of this city. Your silence with regards to the fate of the Watchman and the similarities of your resurrection is what I expect from you, Einherjar, all the rest will be shared with the others at Hydra Company's next briefing."

"What would you have us do, sir?" asked Ajax.

"We shall be like the thanes of old," smiled Thatcher as he stood up from his chair and rapped his armored fist on the table, "And wait in the hall of Heorot to catch Grendel unawares."

"This war has gone sideways on us, marine," said Mahora as he watched the skald walk through the open door. "Time to turn with the tide."

WAR WITHOUT END

Ajax pushed against the ground, his muscles straining for a moment to break the suction of the churning mud before, he could pull himself out. With one hand, he wiped at the thick clumps that clung to his visor while he groped along the bottom of the trench for his pulse rifle. All around him the air was filled with explosions of gunfire and the screams of the dying. Once he had cleared his visor and his fist had found purchase on his rifle, the marine took stock of his immediate surroundings as he tried to clear his head.

He saw another marine struggling to pull himself from the mud and realized that everything around him was covered in Garm spore. The sight of it shook loose his mind and the marine recalled standing on his firing step moments before, methodically hurling bolts into the oncoming swarm of ridgebacks.

The Einherjar had repelled the first wave of ripper drones and gorehounds and with the help of the anti-air battery had all but wiped out a small swarm of shriekers. Ajax realized he must have been knocked from the wall by the spore attack. Indeed, the ridgebacks had waited to launch their spores until they were just inside rifle range. Instead of ordinance arcing over the sky and down into the trench, the ridgebacks charged headlong into the Einherjar guns, dying by the score but pounding their spores into the defenders at such close range that many, like Ajax, had simply been blown backwards into the ditch.

"*Meat!*" roared a voice behind him, and when the marine turned, he saw a ragman getting shakily to his feet. It wasn't until it slid a pistol from its hip holster that Ajax realized it was Boone standing before him.

Ajax snapped his rifle to his shoulder and fired, knowing that if he hesitated even for a second, ragman Boone would kill him with the pistol.

The first round sent the ragman stumbling backwards. The second sent him toppling over from both the force of the impact and the corpse strewn trench that was apt to trip anyone not paying attention. As Boone fell, Ajax realized there were several more marines locked in a violent struggle with each other and in the frenzy of rifle, fist, and trench spike, Ajax could not tell ragman from marine.

Ajax fired one last round at Boone as the ragman struggled to get to his feet, catching his former comrade just under the gap between his chest piece and his lower body plating. When the ragman exploded in a cloud of mud, armor, and gore, Ajax turned back to help the marine behind him.

The marine was standing with his back towards Ajax, still as the grave, despite the bloody madness unfolding in the trench. The marine slowly turned to look at Ajax, his ruined face clearly visible through the shattered visor of his helmet. A bolt had all but vaporized the ragman's head before he could utter the one word the ragmen knew. He collapsed in the mud and lay still.

In the distance, Ajax could see that the marines on that flank were also mired in a civil war against numerous ragmen. Without getting into the thick of the fighting there was no way for Ajax to tell friend from foe and he wasn't about to fire indiscriminately, so he moved back into his firing position.

Rama and Yao were still holding above, each man firing methodically into whatever horrors approached, while Sharif was lost somewhere in the pile of corpses that choked the bottom of the trench, having been slagged by one of the shrieker weapons. The ridgebacks had never attacked in such a manner and the change in tactics had proven radically effective.

Up and down the trench line a sizeable number of the marines who had not already been transformed into ragmen were struggling to deal with those who had and only a few men were left on the firing line.

Ajax joined his comrades on the line and saw what was coming for them. The ridgebacks, their spores now spent, were careening towards the trench, heedless of the grievous damage being done to them. To the marine, the ridgebacks were similar to the long extinct rhinoceros, only blended with the peculiar insect and reptile features common to all Garm.

Each of them had what could only be described as a cannon barrel jutting up from their backs, hence their name among the grunts as ridgebacks. They had thin chitin armor over their bodies, but not in the kind of thickness sported by the gorehounds or ripper drones, which was a meager blessing.

Ajax knew that if even one reached the trench it would exact a heavy toll. Each creature had several horns and scything chitin blades mounted on its head and shoulders that they could use to terrible effect.

"Go for the legs!" came the voice of Jarl Mahora over the command channel. "Every one that falls is a pile of blades and muscle to blunt the charge! Full-auto!"

Ajax did as ordered and thumbed his fire selector over to full-auto. The marine braced himself and cut loose, rapid firing bolt after bolt at the veritable forest of limbs that pounded across the ground towards him.

At first, the marine had been incredulous about the call for full-auto, and then he realized the simple genius of the tactic. While the methodical approach was best for efficient killing, even the sniper, Hart, would have been hard pressed to score a clean hit on the swiftly moving limbs of the beasts with enough speed to slow their advance.

The marine gave a shout of exaltation as he sprayed rounds into the creatures, watching as some of his bolts found their mark. When the bolts hit, they blew huge chunks of the ridgeback's leg away, sometimes even severing the limb entirely. As each of the great beasts toppled over those beside and behind stumbled or fell.

The magazine clicked empty and Ajax vented the heat as he swapped in a fresh carbon mag. The marine saw that some of the ridgebacks indeed had been tripped, impaled, or both by their fallen comrades, and much of the swarm had become a confused mess.

As Ajax brought his rifle up again he realized the awful truth. Mahora's tactic would have worked beautifully had there just been more rifles on the line. They could have stopped the enemy charge and then gone back to selective fire to finish them off. As it was, there were just too few men left in the fight, and after the initial carnage, the remaining ridgebacks were plowing over their wounded comrades and nearing the trench.

Ajax could see WarGarm lurking amidst the ridgeback swarm and knew that this stage of the battle was lost. There was no time left to retreat to the second parallel and for a moment Ajax held his fire and simply looked at the oncoming wave of death. Once again, the Garm had willingly sacrificed the lives of thousands in a suicidal series of attacks, only this time the marines might not be able to rally.

"*First parallel is lost! Deploy Blackouts and blow the connecting lines!*" ordered Mahora, and Ajax knew that the jarl saw the same defeat looming, "If they want in they'll have to come over the top! Make them pay for it marines!"

No sooner had the order come than Rama was blasted from the firestep by a high velocity spore globule. Apparently, a few of the ridgebacks weren't as empty as it seemed, and Ajax was again covered in the fetid substance. Yao kept firing, though Ajax could tell that the man was praying that his fellow marine wouldn't turn.

"I'm with you," said Ajax and then turned his rifle against the enemy, spraying a volley of bolts through the wave of alien flesh that descended upon them.

"If we lose the trench permanently they won't be able to recover our torcs," observed Yao as he vented his rifle and slapped in a fresh magazine. "They'll have to bring us back without any memories of this fight."

"That's happened to us all before," responded Ajax as he vented and reloaded, "Doesn't mean we won't be ourselves again."

"Can't say I wouldn't mind forgetting this one," said Yao as he raised his rifle, "It's about to get nasty."

The two men emptied their weapons once more, their combined fire making a withering curtain of bolts that left many beasts thrashing and bloody on the scrabble ground.

Ajax cursed as his rifle jammed when he attempted to vent. He knew that if he didn't get it cleared the trapped heat would melt the gun's inner workings. The marine knelt upon the fire step and produced his multi-tool, scrambling to clear the weapon. Just as he pulled the breach open, venting the incredible interior heat of the weapon, there was a sickening crunch sound next to him.

Ajax looked up just in time to see the massive head of a ridgeback burying its horns into Yao as it hurled itself over the lip of the trench.

Seven hundred pounds of slavering alien beast plummeted down the side of the trench wall and tumbled to the bottom, leaving a wet smear of blood and armor as Yao went with it. Ajax stood and leveled his rifle upon no man's land only to see several more ridgebacks approaching.

"*Meat!*" howled a voice behind him and armored hands grasped Ajax by the legs and pulled hard.

The marine lost his footing and smacked into the bottom of the firestep as he was pulled off the trench wall. He looked back and saw that Rama had become a ragman, his helmet and armor cracked by the impact of the spores, making his infection swift. Below them, the first ridgeback was getting to its feet, though a great shadow loomed over Ajax, and another ridgeback sailed over the trench. The creature's bulk carried it nearly to the edge of the opposite lip of the trench, but it landed just short and slammed into the far wall.

Ajax found himself screaming at the sight of it all. With one hand holding the bottom of the firestep and the other his rifle, he began shooting. He fired wildly, emptying his magazine on full-auto into the bodies of the thrashing ridgebacks. By the time his gun clicked dry he'd reduced the creatures, and the corpses they'd landed upon, into a thick soup of mud and smoking carnage.

"*Meat!*" shouted ragman Rama as he lashed out with his trench spike over and over, trying to drive the tip through the joints in Ajax's thigh armor.

The marine let go of the firestep and the two opponents fell into the mess at the bottom of the trench. Ajax landed on top of his enemy, using his weight to hold the raving lunatic in place, pinning one arm and pressing down on its chest.

The ragman stabbed with his spike again, but thankfully, Ajax managed to angle his shoulder so that the point glanced off his ceramic armor. The marine had no time to reach for his own spike, as he could feel the thunderous impacts of more ridgebacks filling the trench, so he shoved the breach of his pulse rifle against the ragman's shattered visor. When Ajax released the catch, the pulse rifle vented all the heat built up by the full-auto bursts. At point-blank range, it burned out the ragman's eyes. The enemy was blinded and in sufficient shock from the pain that it allowed Ajax to draw his own trench spike and drive it down through the ragman's eye socket and into his spore-riddled brain.

That made two of his comrades he'd had to kill today, and it took everything Ajax had left to stand back up. Explosions rocked the trench and he knew that what was left of Hydra Company was holding the second parallel and had now blown the connecting trenches. There would be no way to reach the parallel without crossing no man's land. He found himself wondering if the rest of the Einherjar front had been attacked with this level of ferocity and new battle tactics or if once more Trench 16 had withstood the worst of it.

An inhuman roar sounded in the chaos. The marine turned to see a ridgeback barreling down the trench, using its horns to plow a path for itself by swinging it back and forth.

The marine scrambled to find a weapon, splashing through the carnage as he desperately fumbled to get his hands around Rama's discarded rifle. He fell back against the wall of the trench and squeezed the trigger, only to find that poor Rama had been in the process of a reload when he'd been hit by the spores. The ridgeback was seconds from him when out of the blind corner of a connecting tunnel came a cloud of bolts that all but shredded the beast.

Ajax threw himself to the ground near the other side of the trench as the ruined bulk of the ridgeback, carried by sheer momentum, collapsed in a heap just short of where he'd been standing.

He lay where he had fallen, half-covered in carnage and mud. A Blackout emerged from the connecting tunnel, his machine pistol smoldering from the murderous salvo that had taken out the Ridgeback.

A WarGarm came rushing down the trench, spitting clouds of spikes from its weapons as it advanced. The Blackout rolled under the wave of fire, avoiding all but two of the spikes that the marine could see. As Ajax watched, the Blackout deftly sliced the WarGarm apart before finally succumbing to the toxins being pumped into his system by the two spikes in his body. Other WarGarm either leapt across the wide trench or climbed in and out of the obstacle, all of them focused on pressing the attack to the second parallel.

The Einherjar flares, both first and second wave, had all but faded away, and now the trench was growing steadily darker, ever more reliant upon the handful of LED lights that were undamaged.

Ajax risked a glance towards the other end of the trench and saw only heaps of bodies. In the distance, he could hear gunfire and knew that the marines on the second parallel were fighting to hold the line against the WarGarm.

Again, the enemy had forced the marines to spend their strength against lesser swarms so that the WarGarm could close in for the killing blow. That attack had failed last time, though the ploy with the ridgebacks had truly been a devastating one. There were few marines left to hold the second parallel, even bolstered as they were by the handful of skald commandos in the field.

The skalds were tasked with bringing down the forward observer so they would be busy monster hunting. Skald Thatcher had taken to calling the new creature Grendel, and the name had stuck, even if, to Ajax, the slithering beast would always be the observer. Something in its eyes made him feel as if it could see right through him, its gaze piercing his flesh and laying bare every memory or secret he'd ever had.

Thatcher had taken the Watchman's place, and hoped to draw the enemy to him, since the Watchman was its first key victim.

Hart, the sniper, as the only other man to see the creature, actually wound it and live, was with the commandos, accompanied by a skald escort, defending Trench 16. They would be out there, stalking the beast even as it stalked them, if Grendel came to this area.

Ajax fervently hoped that they were successful.

Thoughts of the observer made Ajax realize he was the only living thing in sight. The trench suddenly felt more menacing and dangerous than when it was filled with vicious combat. Bodies were everywhere, but no more enemies poured over the side of the trench, and no marines fought to hold the line. The marine's instincts screamed at him to run, in any direction, so long as it was out of this ditch, and it took everything the marine had left to simply stand.

Ajax took up the pulse rifle and out of a habit, he ejected the carbon mag and tapped it to settle what inert ammunition remained. He estimated he had about half a magazine left as he slotted it in and racked the slide of the rifle to chamber the first projectile. From the sound of it the fighting between the WarGarm and the marines was reaching its conclusion, one way or the other.

The marine carefully picked his way through the piles of bodies that clogged the trench, slowly making his way towards the nearest chain-fire emplacement. He knew from the trench layout that it was nearly sixty meters away and in the dying light it would be a treacherous journey. Then again, Ajax thought to himself, what else was the last man standing to do?

A deep rumbling sound reached the marine's ears as he finally came upon the thin ladder that led up to the chain-fire. The marine slung the pulse rifle over his shoulder and started climbing, noticing that the ladder itself had begun to shake. Ajax made it to the top and pulled himself onto the small gun platform.

The two gunners were dead, both riddled with messy holes and covered in the splattered bodies of the grubs that were fired from the horrific weapons of the gorehounds. No matter how many times he saw it, the sight of the grub filled corpses of his fallen comrades threatened to make him vomit. The marine was shaking so badly that he had to grab the handle of the chain-fire just to stand. It was only when the shaking didn't stop that he realized it wasn't him at all, but the world itself.

Ajax looked up from the ruined bodies of his brothers and his gaze was filled with the breath stealing sight of the UltraGarm.

The living battle tanks were so huge that they were easily two and three times as massive as the ridgebacks, reminding him of what a cockroach war drone might look like if it was the size of an elephant. There were wide scythe blades of chitin extending from the thick jaws of the creature, giving it an elephantine look, two pairs of blades, along with innumerable spines and armor plating covering the beast. There were three of them, and the impact of their hooves upon the ground shook the entire trench.

No sooner had Ajax laid eyes on them than one of the UltraGarm burst apart in an explosion of super-heated gas that almost knocked Ajax over where he stood. The sky was filled with skyrocketing meat and bodily fluids that splattered everywhere as they fell back to the ground.

A split second after the beast died Ajax heard the unique report of a tank cannon. He caught sight of two heavy battle tanks in pursuit of the two remaining UltraGarm. While he was happy to see the tank, the marine could not fathom why the UltraGarm seemed to be fleeing from battle, as that was not at all the Garm way of war.

Suddenly, the two UltraGarm split up. One turned and ran further into no man's land, as if retreating in the direction of the unknown hive ship, while the other charged the trench itself.

The tanks were forced to engage the UltraGarm in no man's land, as the beast was on an intercept course with the tanks unless they deviated.

Before the tanks could engage in combat, Ajax realized what the UltraGarm charging the trench was doing. The great beast changed its angle of approach and swept its wicked tusks through the other chain-fire emplacement defending Trench 16.

As was standard procedure, the marines fired until the weapon locked up, then abandoned it until it either cooled or other marines re-took the trench. Einherjar had been using chain-fires this way since their first deployment as support weapons, especially as they, like the rest of humanity's war machines, were in short supply and growing more difficult to replace as the war ground on.

The UltraGarm's blades sheared the chain-fire into several pieces, rendering the weapon completely useless. There might be parts that could be salvaged, but Trench 16 would be without a second chain-fire until Command sent a re-supply mission with another operational unit from one of the weaponsmith factories deep in human space.

Even if the marines re-took the trench, as Ajax was certain they would, they would stand against the swarm with one less weapon. The Garm had never targeted their weapon systems in the past, so focused were the creatures on rending and consuming the men themselves, that the marines often used that simple oversight to catastrophic effect.

As the UltraGarm roared and shook its head to disentangle itself from some of the mooring cables, Ajax snapped out of his reverie. The marine turned swiftly and thumbed the ignition of the chain-fire, thankful that the gun had lain silent long enough to cool. There was half a carbon block in the ammo hopper and Ajax prayed it was enough to do the job.

The chain-fire snarled to life and the UltraGarm snapped its head around to face the marine's position. There was recognition of a threat in its posture, and Ajax marveled at how clearly it recognized the sound of his weapon. Like the shriekers, he thought, just before leveling the weapon at the charging beast.

Ajax was astounded at how quickly the UltraGarm moved, covering meter after meter in the blink of an eye. His respect for the tank gunners increased as he realized how much skill it must take to hit the creature with a single cannon round. The marine squeezed the trigger and the chain-fire roared as it spat bolts at the oncoming abomination.

The UltraGarm's thick armor allowed it to shrug off most of the bolts, though as it drew near the marine managed to direct his fire at the creature's head. The force of the multitude of impacts knocked the creature's head hard to the side, and Ajax threw his weight behind the gun while still shooting. The marine applied enough force that he swiftly changed the trajectory of the weapon while it was still firing, muscling through the bucking recoil as he re-directed it.

Several bolts slammed into the exposed flesh beneath the joints in the chitin armor protecting the UltraGarm's neck and shoulder. Once those first bolts penetrated, the secondary explosions blasted great chunks of flesh and armor out of the beast. The UltraGarm lost its footing and crashed to the ground, its speed causing the beast to tumble over, while Ajax continued to pepper it with bolts.

When the chain-fire clicked dry and Ajax swiftly stepped away from it and pulled his rifle off his shoulder. He set the rifle to single shot with his fire selector and concentrated on putting precise bolt rounds through the exposed wounds the thrashing beast already had.

It only took four clean hits to finish the beast, which was good, as Ajax only had enough carbon left in his rifle's block to get three more shots off. He was looking at the fallen creature, marveling at how much sheer firepower it had taken to bring just one down when he recalled that there was a second UltraGarm still active.

Ajax gasped in surprise when he looked up, helpless, and saw the second UltraGarm bearing down on him. In the seconds before collision, Ajax could see that the tanks had managed to wound the creature with an indirect hit, but not enough to keep it from its goal. The marine snapped off two ineffectual shots before the creature swung its tremendous head.

The four blades projecting form its mouth tore through the chain-fire and Ajax as the UltraGarm thundered onwards, smashing its armored body into the gun emplacement for good measure.

Ajax sailed through the air. As he collided with the opposite side of the trench, he saw that the lower half of his body was gone, he'd been sheared in two by the UltraGarm's blades.

The last thing he saw was the ravaged body of the dying UltraGarm falling into the trench before it buried him under tons of flesh and armor plating.

ENEMY WITHIN

The ground was the same hard scrabble as every other brackenworld he'd been on, only he couldn't help but recognize the dark pebbles and bits of shale that made Heorot such a gloomy place. The rocks seemed to eat the light, drawing it in and making everything so dim that even flares and LEDs did little to illuminate the grim little world.

Ajax became aware of himself, noticing that he was alone upon a vast landscape which would have been featureless save for the occasional ravine that cut through the ground or stone pillar jutting up from the earth. It was a severe place, with little upon the surface to warrant human occupation.

It was the wind that humanity had come to harvest, made possible only by such harsh conditions. It seemed strange to Ajax that they would fight so hard to hold onto such a fleeting thing as wind, and yet it was the energy that wind created that kept their ships running and their lights shining, and so they fought.

The crunch of booted feet sounded behind him. The warm hands of a woman slid over his tired shoulders and embraced him, making him at once aware of her body pressed against his and the absence of the suit of armor that had become his second skin.

The Valkyrie's presence was soothing. Even in the slicing wind he felt some modicum of peace, never mind that he was crouching upon hard ground, surrounded by the slow churning of rusted windmills and lonely stones cut sharp by the endless winds. She had been his wife once, how could he not have found peace with her near?

Through it all he heard the now familiar bone on bone sound. The Valkyrie turned his face towards hers and nodded as she gently helped him to his feet. This time there was no meat or mead in her hands for him, only the cold feel of his pulse rifle gripped in his hands.

Ajax went through his ritual of ejecting the magazine and tapping it, this time against the gun itself, to settle the carbon block in its casing. He racked the slide and when looked up, the Valkyrie was gone.

Now that he was scanning his surroundings for her, he noticed a dull purple glow in the distant gloom.

He crept towards the light, moving through the desolation surrounding him. He found himself wishing for his armor to protect him from the scouring wind. His body glove did what it could, but without a mask or goggles the marine was weeping from the wind and raw from the micro-abrasions caused by the rock and shale particles in the wind.

Soon, the sound of the windmills had faded into the background. He saw a small ravine leading towards the light, and noticed that it sprang from the base of a particularly large wind cut stone. The marine made his way down into the ravine, taking extra care not to cut himself on the sharp edges of the formation.

The bone on bone sound reached his ears again, though it was much further down the path that the ravine cut through the land leading towards the stone. He kept his pulse rifle at the ready, prepared to ignite it, but keeping the weapon inert for now just to reduce the noise he was making as he approached. It took him a while to move through the ravine, and when he reached the end of it he wasn't sure how much time had passed.

When he emerged, the marine was met with the unmistakable sight of a hive ship. It was the size of a building, and from his education in Garm anatomy he knew that there would be just as much of the ship buried beneath the surface as he could see above it. It was easily the size of a standard warship. He knew that inside it would be hundreds of birthing chambers for the swarm, where organic material harvested would be consumed and turned into nutrients and new flesh for the brood. There would be no storage sacs within the hive ship, for this was one of the assault breeds. That much he could tell in the gloom. The extinction fleet would dispatch warships to eliminate local resistance, and only then would it bring the harvester ships.

What struck the marine, other than the novelty of being this close to a hive ship for the first time in his long career as a soldier, was the awkward shape of it. The longer he observed the hive ship the more he realized that it was quite unlike anything he'd ever seen. It was similar to the rest of the Garm swarm, but upon careful scrutiny he began to see details that set it apart.

This one seemed to be more bloated and armored at the base, while the jagged spires that rose above the cracked planet surface were dotted with gas vents and what appeared to be gun emplacements.

The bone on bone sound returned, and this time, he could positively feel the eyes of Grendel upon him. There was even a smell that was familiar, a cloying musk that stank of death and rotting fruit. It was here with him, somewhere in the ravine, and it was stalking him. There was a palpable sense of fury in the air, like a kind of static electricity that he could almost taste and suddenly Ajax knew he'd seen something he wasn't supposed to.

His attempt at recon had gone too far, been too greedy, and he had been discovered. The marine had no idea where he would go, but he knew that he had to get out of the ravine. Something told him that if he died *here*, it would be permanent.

The marine moved slowly back down into the ravine, then, as the sound of the beast came near, he sprinted away. He heard the inhuman roar behind him and the sound of it slithering after him. Ajax pumped his legs and gave it everything he had to stay ahead of the creature. With every passing second he became certain that to die *here*, was to die for good.

He had to speak of what he'd seen.

He did not know his way back to Heorot from here, but he was sure he could at least make it to the windmills. Perhaps from there he could better defend against the creature, as it would have to come at him across open ground.

Grendel suddenly lashed out at him. Out of the corner of his eye, Ajax saw the barbed end of its tail pound into the stone wall of the ravine mere inches from his body. Up ahead, he could see the end of the ravine, where the rock formation made a sort of rough natural stair he could climb. There was no way he would be able to ascend without being taken by the creature. The marine ignited his rifle and was bolstered by the sound of his weapon coming online. He might be the prey, much as he disliked accepting that, but he was not without claws of his own.

Ajax fired from the hip as he ran, punching bolts into the walls on either side of the ravine. Shards of rock ravaged his body. Ajax had to buy himself at least a few seconds, so he thumbed the fire selector over to full-auto.

As the marine hit the first step he threw himself forward, spinning his body and slamming his back into the steps painfully, but swiftly giving himself a field of fire on the ravine behind him. For the first time, Ajax could see the nightmare coming after him and Grendel was terrible to behold.

The sight of it filled his imagination with images of giant centipedes and snakes and all manner of Garm creatures he'd seen thus far, and he nearly passed out from the mental shock of Grendel's presence.

The creature's undulating body was a pale sickly color and layered with pulsing rolls of mucus covered flesh. It's back and shoulders bristled with hundreds of twitching spines and its sides were festooned with several pairs of claw tipped, disturbingly humanoid arms.

He squeezed the trigger both out of fear and desperation. Thankfully the pulse rifle roared in his hands, and the deafening report of the full-auto weapon in the confines of the ravine snapped him out of the hypnosis that had gotten him killed the first time he met the creature.

The beast screamed and was lost to sight as the ravine was filled with clouds of spore and a hurricane of shattered stone shrapnel.

Ajax fired until his weapon seized up and he knew he had to vent it before the internal parts melted. He scampered up the side of the ravine, caring little for how many times he cut his hands and legs as he ascended. The wind was a harsh companion that met him once he reached the top, but he was happy to have it instead of the thing below.

The marine ran, pushing himself to the very limits of his endurance as he made his way towards the windmills. He was out of ammunition, and unless the Valkyrie woman had more magazines he was unsure how he would fight, but he knew he had to reach them.

Ajax ran until his sides burned from the effort, and his sight was blurry from sweat and grit. It became a struggle to put one foot in front of the other, but he thought he would make it until a brilliant light hit his eyes and blinded him.

DISTRICT 9

The siege had gone poorly and the Einherjar trench network had been overrun. The corpses of man and beast had been taken into the darkness by the Garm scavengers, great shelled beasts that resembled land-roving octopi more than anything else, raked up with their many tentacles to be taken to the Garm ships, providing more meat for the breeding chambers of the hive.

Armor One had pulled back after sustaining multiple casualties and exhausting their supply of ammunition and fuel.

Chain-fires and rifles spat bolts at shriekers and WarGarm that harassed the circumference of the city's battlements.

Heorot was assaulted from within by ragmen who transformed after sustained bombardment by ridgeback swarms that surrounded the small city.

The walls of District 9 were breached by the suicidal charges of the UltraGarm, even though the living battle tanks were slaughtered in the process and now swarms of ripper drones were pouring through.

In the gloom, it was impossible to guess at the size of the swarms that came screaming towards Heorot from all sides. Atmospheric conditions on the planet prevented Bright Lance from launching attack fighter sorties from low orbit.

Skald Thatcher had taken the Watchman's place in the Tower, and while he performed admirably, the forces of the Garm were seemingly inexhaustible.

"*Shieldwall!*" bellowed Jarl Mahora over the company channel. Across District 9 the sound of interlocking mobile flak boards slamming into each other could be heard.

Ajax bent his knees and hefted his own board, holding it in front of himself, his left arm turned at a ninety-degree angle to keep the board positioned where it would protect him from mid-calf to neck.

He slotted the barrel of his pulse rifle through the makeshift gun port that had been cut out of the top right section of the shield.

The flak boards were intended to be temporary defenses used in rapid deployment scenarios, where marines could erect a hard point to defend and then move on after a single engagement. When the war with the Garm transformed into a bloody trench grind, the board had been relegated to reinforcing trench perimeters. It was a desperate ploy to use them in a street fight, but with the trench networks overrun there was little choice, they had to use what they could to re-take the city.

The marine knew that once the ripper drones reach them, the flak boards would only keep the alien killers at bay for one or perhaps two direct hits before shattering into pieces.

Upon awakening from his troubled resurrection dreams, Ajax and his comrades were met with the news that two hive ships had smashed their way past the blockade and made planetfall, although one of them was thought to have been badly damaged.

The hive ships had appeared without warning, approaching the planet directly, seeming to twist out of the darkness between the stars as they were wont to do. Bright Lance had scrambled starfighters and brought its own heavy guns into the conflict, wiping out the starborne escort creatures that sought to defend the hive ships.

Though the miasma of the planet's atmosphere prevented Bright Lance from pinpointing the hive ships, it was clear that they'd already disgorged their initial swarms and were busy breeding more. Swarm after swarm crashed into the Einherjar defenses, and the forces of humanity had been pushed out of the trench network.

The walls of Heorot were stout. They had been built to handle the scouring winds that made the planet so profitable for the windmill operations. Once the Einherjar had arrived and begun their trench network, more reinforcements had been added to the small city, and now it stood as a potent secondary line of defense.

Or so it had been thought.

Sharif stepped up directly behind Ajax and held his board over the marine's head at an angle that would provide cover from any shots or caustic fluids fired from above, while still giving Ajax enough of a line of sight to observe the battlefield and fire his weapon.

The marine sighted down the length of his rifle and waited, knowing that any second now, the first wave of ripper drones would be upon them.

It was lucky that Hydra Company was here to hold the district, thought Ajax as he flexed his fingers, the unit had been pulled out of Trench 16 after the last engagement. They had sustained ninety percent casualties and with so many in the body forge, the company was the strongest unit not already positioned on the line.

"I feel like I just drank an ocean of Boone's homebrew before a forced march through the desert," complained Rama as he crouched in the shieldwall next to Ajax, who was suddenly very thankful that, by some small miracle, marines had no memories of their time as ragmen. Better not to recall killing your comrades and being killed by them in turn.

"Idris had to dilute the equilibrium solutions to resurrect so many of us so quickly," pointed out Boone, who stood behind Rama, his own shield locked with Sharif's, "And we've only been alive for about an hour, we all feel it, brother."

A single shot rang out, the unique signature of the sound identifying it as a high velocity sniper round, and the marines knew that the bloodshed was about to begin.

"WarGarm moving up to support ripper swarm, one down, looks like at least two more incoming," crackled Hart's voice over the channel. "Be advised, the swarm is dividing its approach, rooftops are in play."

Ajax took a deep breath and let it out slowly as he prepared for the attack. Hart was on overwatch somewhere above and behind the shieldwall. The sniper was, again, once of the few marines to survive the most recent engagement at Trench 16.

Grendel had once again slipped through their preparations and managed to avoid the multitudes of skalds and snipers who hunted it. Ajax had only been resurrected for a short time and had been thrown into combat scant minutes after making the report of his resurrection dream to Thatcher and Jarl Mahora, but even he had heard the rumors going around that the beast had murdered a full tank crew. Command was refusing to make anything official, and that made Ajax more certain that it was indeed true.

If Grendel had slain and harvested the brains of an entire tank crew, then based on what they knew so far, it was likely that intelligence gained by the observer was why the Garm had been able to inflict unprecedented casualties on Armor One just a few hours ago.

The marine was shaken from his reverie by the sudden, deafening sound of a chorus of inhuman voices risen in a feral howl. Moments later the sounds of scuttling claws and snapping mandibles preceded the first of the rippers as they rounded the corner.

Heorot was a circular city, making each urban block something of a triangle divided into smaller sections by various roads and alleyways. Hydra Company had the entire district covered at each cross-section. If the Garm wanted to spread from District 9 to anywhere else, they'd have to get past the shieldwalls of Hydra.

"Weapons free!" shouted Jarl Mahora. His order sent bolts snarling from the muzzles of rifles and streaking through the short distance between the marines and the swarm.

Ajax squeezed the trigger of his rifle and couldn't grinning savagely as his first bolt struck home, sending pieces of a shattered ripper drone splattering across its brood. The marine moved to his next target and fired, the first round punching through the creature's knee. As the beast fell, the marine's second round went wide, though as tightly packed as the drones were, thanks to the compact urban environment, missing one beast only meant that his round fatally struck another.

Despite the temptation to go full-auto, Ajax knew better. His weapon would doubtless overheat and it was faster to swap out magazines than it was to wait on a weapon to cool down while the enemy bore down on him. He fired his tenth round and paused to vent his weapon, only the years of experience fighting the Garm swarms giving him the discipline to hold his fire despite the swarm drawing ever closer.

The marine raised his rifle once more and continued to fire, taking note that Sharif and Boone had both started firing. Ajax risked a glance upwards and saw that scores of drones were skittering over the low rooftops of the buildings.

When there was a sudden, powerful impact against his shield, Ajax turned his head to see that the roadway in front of him was now teeming with gorehounds.

"*Frak the collateral! Grenades!*" boomed the voice of Mahora. Ajax realized that the other shieldwalls must be encountering a similar situation.

The bulk of the ripper drones had gone over the rooftops, with only just enough of them on the ground level to soak up bolt rounds until the gorehounds were close enough to use their hideous grub launchers.

"So much for District 9," huffed Boone as he cut loose with his grenade launcher, pumping explosive ordinance into the wall of alien flesh that galloped across the ground towards them.

Ajax pointed his rifle upwards and sent a ripper drone's corpse spiraling off the roof and into the street with a well-aimed bolt. He could see that plenty of the rippers were being gunned down, but it was impossible to stem the tide. He knew that in a matter of moments the marines would be fighting enemies in front and behind.

His shield was dripping with the broken and wriggling bodies of a clutch of grubs that had been fired at him by one of the gorehounds and he knew that his shield would only withstand one or two more such blasts.

The grenades from Boone tore through the ranks of the gorehounds, sending many of them sprawling and screaming as they died from a combination of the explosion and their own grubs eating them from the inside out. Many of those that didn't die from the grenades directly were smashed by debris from buildings that were rocked by the explosions. While Boone hustled to re-fill his cylinder, more of the enemy galloped over the corpses of the fallen, spewing grubs as they came, and the shieldwall shuddered from the impact.

Ajax grunted as he held himself firm against the tempest of tiny impacts, keenly aware of the trench spike he held in his shield hand and knowing that it wouldn't be long until he had to use it. The second the impacts stopped, Ajax leveled his rifle at the swarm and fired. He had to force himself to take the time to aim for precise shots, as the gorehounds were sufficiently armored to turn away indirect hits. He could still feel and hear the impacts of ripper drones as their bodies smacked into the ground.

Yao was behind both Sharif and Boone, flanked by other rifles that were not encumbered by shields, and it was they who kept the ripper swarms from descending upon the shieldwall, though the enemy gained ground with every passing moment.

Men began to scream and die as the gorehounds pressed the attack, their withering hail of grubs finally chewing holes out of the shieldwall.

"Lock and advance, marines!" ordered Mahora, and this time Ajax heard his voice both in the channel and somewhere behind him. The proximity of the jarl himself gave Ajax a boost of confidence as well as adrenaline. In a way, the jarl was like a WarGarm for the human side, as the force of his personality and the unit's awareness of his combat prowess made the men naturally gather around him and fight more ferociously in his presence.

"Hooah!" grunted the marines as every man on the shieldwall took a step forward, shouting it again as they took another. As moved, the holes in the shieldwall locked into place once more, the gaps made by the enemy fire closed as fallen marines were left on the ground behind the formation. The gorehounds were taken by surprise at the sudden advance combined with a counter-salvo of deadly bolt rounds, and the swarm's advance faltered.

"Hooah!" shouted Ajax, taking another step forward, squeezing the trigger of his rifle again and again as he and the marines around him shouted.

The gorehounds, like all the Garm, were supposedly incapable of retreat, but with their forward momentum broken they were not able to pour on the coordinated fire that they had moments before.

A gorehound near the front hosed Ajax and Rama's shields with grubs and the marines were forced to drop them as the voracious ammunition chewed their already battered flak boards to pieces.

Boone responded with another grenade salvo, his ordinance set to airburst, while he and Sharif stepped over their comrades to protect them with their own shields. The shrapnel and gore from the explosions hammered the shields but did not break them.

Rama and Ajax let the marines move another step ahead of them and then stood to their full height, firing their rifles over the heads of their comrades and into the broken swarm.

The shieldwall advanced. The marines had now come far enough that they were walking over the bodies of the enemy. Ajax slammed the point of his trench knife into the skull of a wounded gorehound while Rama finished off a weakly thrashing ripper drone.

Mahora shouted for the wall to continue to advance, and as they did, their rifles dropped the last of the gorehhounds. Ajax drove his knife under the body armor of another wounded gorehound, taking extra care not to tear open its ammunition sacs, and then Yao fired behind them.

"Rippers flanking us," observed Yao from his vantage point behind the shieldwall, the man's rifle barking once more as if to drive his point home.

Ajax and Rama turned their guns away from the grisly scene in front of the shieldwall and added their firepower to Yao's. Ajax could see that several ripper drones had indeed managed to move around to flank the shieldwall. They were close, too close, and Ajax knew it was about to get messy.

He gunned down a ripper drone as it charged him, and then saw from his peripheral vision that another was scampering over a low rooftop to his left. He turned on the balls of his feet, raising his rifle just in time to punch a bolt round into the creature's chest. The beast exploded wetly in mid-leap, showering Ajax and his comrades in gore, distracting them long enough for a second one to land in their midst.

The rippers were generally cannon fodder, disposable creatures hurled into the Einherjar guns to create opportunities for other, deadlier organisms to close in for the kill. The problem was that the ripper drones were deadly on their own, and being creatures made of muscle and blade, they could wreak havoc if they got close enough.

The ripper drone screamed, ignorant of everything but its hunger, and it swept its blades through Yao's armor with tremendous force. The marine's rifle and right arm fell to the ground as the rest of him was pinned underneath the gnashing teeth and rending claws of the ripper.

Rama shoved the barrel of his rifle under the ripper's jaw and squeezed the trigger, turning the drone's head into a blossom of meat and blood. In an instant, two of the three rifles were no longer firing at the clutch of drones rushing up the alleyway, and Ajax had no choice but to go full-auto. He sprayed the full contents of his magazine down the mouth of the alley, and while his attack turned the drones into so much quivering meat his pulse rifle seized up from the lack of proper venting.

"High right!" shouted Rama from somewhere behind him, but without a working rifle Ajax did the only thing he could do.

The marine gripped the body of his rifle and pushed it into the air to his right without even looking, knowing full well that clawed death was descending upon him.

The ripper drone slammed into the marine, the weight of the horrid thing driving them both to the ground. Ajax held his rifle between himself and the ripper and that fact alone saved his life. The beast's jaws were wrapped around the rifle, having bitten the weapon nearly in half, but better the rifle than the marine. Ajax roared and shoved his trench spike into the beast, ramming the point of it up through the creature's thorax and into whatever passed for a ripper drone's brain. The creature shuddered for a moment and Ajax wondered if he'd missed its central nervous system, then it ceased to struggle and its body went slack.

Ajax heaved with all his might and shoved the corpse off so that he could scramble to his feet. With his rifle destroyed, the gore-slick spike was his only weapon and he knew that he wouldn't be so lucky as to kill a ripper drone with it a second time. Thankfully, in a grim sort of way, Rama had recovered Yao's rifle and pitched it over to the unarmed marine. Ajax slotted a fresh magazine into the weapon and surveyed the scene before him.

Only humans stood upon the intersection of road and alley and though they'd suffered more casualties than he'd realized, Ajax saw that victory, at least for the moment, was theirs.

The ripper drones couldn't mount enough of a flanking attack to disrupt the shieldwall and the last of the gorehounds were being put down.

Jarl Mahora stepped away from the formation and began giving orders, his commands made more potent for the gore that dripped from his trench spike as he gestured with it.

"Police your ammo and form a square," ordered Mahora, then added, "We might have stopped them for now, but we all know they'll be back. If another Garm wave arrives before the engineers can get the wall repaired we'll be in for another brawl."

The marines rushed to prepare themselves, and within a few minutes they stood in a square formation, each man with a fresh magazine in his pulse rifle. They'd all heard Hart mention two WarGarm driving the swarms, but so far, they had not appeared. It was unlike the WarGarm to abandon the attack, unless the swarm required them for more urgent purpose elsewhere. Each man knew this, and as if to answer their silent question, a voice crackled over the command channel.

"Grendel just took out the jarl of Manticore Company, multiple sightings confirmed in District 10," came Skald Thatcher's voice over the company channel. "Available elements converge!"

"Ajax, Rama, Ford, and Silas, break away and get yourselves over to District 10 and support the skalds," barked Mahora as he pointed to each man in turn with his bloody spike. "Hart, drop overwatch and join them."

"But, jarl, the WarGarm might still be in 9," protested Hart over the channel.

"Step to it, Einherjar, the rest of us will handle the WarGarm if they decide to make a move," interrupted Mahora. "You lads have a monster to kill."

GRENDEL

Ajax and his small squad of marines rushed through the narrow streets of Heorot, their built-in squad beacon buzzing as it indicated their position relative to the signal being broadcast by Skald Thatcher's command module. In the distance, they could hear the sounds of battle and reports indicated that the swarm's strength was waning. The Garm never retreated and even though they had failed to seize the city they continued to attack, each time with successively smaller numbers.

It was a testament to the weapons and combat prowess of the Einherjar that such a great swarm had been shattered against their defenses, Ajax reflected as he moved through the uncannily silent streets that made up the outskirts of District 10. With two hive ships adding their strength to the swarm it seemed a miracle that Heorot had not yet been overrun.

Every point on the wall had been sorely tested by the enemy, but the walls of Heorot stood firm except for District 9. Manticore Company had been stationed in District 10, and by all accounts had been defending their bit of wall with brutal efficiency. Radio chatter made it clear that despite the loss of Jarl Grummond, the warriors of Manticore were fighting hard to finish off the scattered and desperate assaults of the broken swarm. The civilians of Heorot had been moved behind makeshift barricades beneath the shadow of the capital building, so the streets were empty, and yet Ajax felt as if they were suddenly filled with a palpable malice.

Rama seemed to sense it, too, and the marines paused at the mouth of an alleyway to exchange glances before proceeding.

"Do you feel that?" asked Ford, flexing his fingers on the grip of his rifle, scanning an empty street and seeming rather unsatisfied with what he found, or more, what he did not find.

"Grendel is here," whispered Hart through their ear-beads. The marines looked up to see the sniper crouching on the edge of a rooftop above them, training his sniper rifle deeper into the abandoned district.

They could hear the echoes of crisp reports, the chopped pulse assault rifles carried by the skalds, and each man tensed as he brought his weapon up.

"I can see two skalds moving across the rooftops, Thatcher, too," reported Hart as his rifle tracked to the left. "I can't tell whether they're attempting to herd the beast or simply keep it from slipping away."

"What do we do?" asked Silas. "They called for available units. Are we just supposed to flood the area with rifles?"

"Hart, you're on the skald channel, right?" asked Ajax, having a feeling that the secretive warriors had given the sniper access to their exclusive communication network. When the sniper nodded, he said, "Give them our grid coordinates. If they can flush it towards us we can engage. Once we do, throw the green flare so Thatcher knows we've got it occupied. Maybe you and the skalds can bring it down before we're all dead."

"I had a sinking suspicion that was your plan," scoffed Rama warmly, his gallows humor seemingly undiluted despite his repeated and increasingly grisly deaths. "But how are we going to make sure it doesn't just move around us?"

"This thing is smart, it's learning our ways of fighting, figuring out our weapons," said Ajax. "Maybe we can use that against it."

Minutes later, Hart had disappeared, slinking off into the gloom to find a better overwatch position. The marines were gritting their teeth and waiting for the enemy to approach.

Ajax and the others had set up booby traps that covered the roads and alleys leading into a small plaza. At the center of the plaza was the first windmill device to be built on Heorot and the area was something of a historical site for the once burgeoning community.

The skalds were getting closer, the steady crackle of their small arms fire getting louder, and the marines knew that soon the beast would be upon them.

If Grendel was aware of even cursory facts about the weapons of the Einherjar, then it would recognize the thin wires stretched across the roads and alleyways. It would see the hastily shaped charges made from det-putty that each soldier carried. Usually, it was used to make trenches quickly by blowing out patterns in the ground that would then be shaped by shovel and board, though they made handy booby trap devices as well.

It took everything Ajax had to avoid telling the men about what he knew concerning Grendel's ability to consume the brains of the slain. Thankfully, Hart's association with the skalds, and the inevitable barracks gossip about Ajax having met personally with Skald Thatcher, gave the two marines enough clout to pass the plan off without having to reveal what they knew of the beast they hunted. Ajax reasoned that if Grendel had consumed knowledge of not only the Watchman, but the recon scouts, then it must know how to recognize the traps, what he was gambling on was that the creature wouldn't know the difference between a well-hidden device and one put on display.

Ajax and Rama held their rifles at the ready, each man crouching behind the low wall that surrounded the historical windmill. Above them, on the left and right, perched on rooftops, were Silas and Ford, with Hart somewhere in the darkness. Ajax knew that Grendel would come here the moment he'd seen the windmill. He remembered it from his resurrection dream, and from the moment he first encountered this creature he had determined that there were no coincidences on Heorot. Something big was happening here, and this fight with Grendel had become the entire Garm war. He was sure that the beast would attack and slaughter him and the other marines, but if they could buy the skalds or Hart even a single chance at taking the beast down it would be a win.

Ajax worked to calm himself. The gunshots of the skalds grew ever closer, signaling that the beast was upon them. The bone on bone sound reached his ears and he felt as if he were once again in the resurrection dream. He wished he had Kora at his side as he did then. She had always given him a reservoir of strength to draw on and he could have used some of that in this moment. Suddenly, three skalds appeared on the rooftops ahead of the marines, yet the one alleyway they had not booby-trapped was empty.

At first, Ajax was incredulous that the beast had not moved the way it had been driven, for surely even Grendel could not have avoided the skalds once the elite commandos had the measure of it.

Suddenly Silas cried out, and Ajax snapped his head upwards just in time to see the marine's body soaring through the air, trailing blood and viscera as it went. Across the street, Ford fired his pulse rifle and soon a shower of debris cascaded from the side of the building where Silas had once been positioned.

Ajax could hear Ford uttering panicked curses as the marine fired, the brief glimpse of Grendel slaying his comrade having been sufficiently disturbing to unhinge him. Ajax tracked Ford's line of fire in the hopes that he could catch a piece of the enemy in his sights, though in the gloom there was little that met his eye beyond gray buildings and shadows.

"There!" shouted Rama just before he squeezed the trigger of his own weapon to send several bolt rounds shrieking through the air, tearing huge chunks of metal and concrete out of a squat building off to the left.

Ajax swung his rifle around, but before he could find his target, a projectile bit into the low wall he crouched behind. He heard it before it struck as it made a whining sound, as if air passed through parts of it to give the projectile an audible signature, or perhaps it was another example of the living bullets that the Garm sometimes fired, either way Ajax felt it too terrible to contemplate overmuch. It appeared to be a spine of sorts, much like that fired by the WarGarm. It had splintered upon impact to reveal that it was filled with a fluid that was already melting a significant section of the wall into caustic slag.

The marine let his instincts take over, trusting that his years of combat would lead his aim to the enemy if he could just quiet his mind and calm his nerves. This was a monumental task in the heat of battle, though one that every Einherjar trained ceaselessly to accomplish.

The whine met his ears again as another projectile whisked past his shoulder. From behind him Ajax could hear Rama screaming horribly. He let it fall away from his awareness, for this was certainly not the first time he had fought on while his friends died all around him.

The marine caught a glimpse of Grendel in the shadows, its sickly pale chitin reflecting for a moment the green light of a signal flare that streaked into the sky to illuminate the plaza. Ajax squeezed the trigger and very nearly struck the creature, missing by a mere inch, and just as quickly as it appeared, the beast was gone, its escape masked by the shower of debris from the bolt's impact against the building.

More shots rang out as the skalds leapt off the rooftops and sprinted across the plaza. They had more refined optics than the average Einherjar grunt, and Ajax was sure they could see something more of the beast than he'd been able to. He ducked back behind what was left of the wall as the skald's line of fire passed over his position, giving him a chance to take account of Rama's condition.

The spine had pierced the man's right shoulder, and the liquids inside the projectile had neatly melted away the tissues and armor connecting his arm to his body. The marine was alive and desperately injecting himself with basic stims from his personal kit. Ajax recovered Rama's weapon and swapped out the magazines as one of the skalds vaulted the low wall in hot pursuit of the creature. Rama grimaced but nodded in thanks as Ajax pressed the grip of the pulse rifle into the wounded marine's hand.

Grendel roared and Ajax caught sight of it crashing through the doorway of a building, chased by raking fire from the skalds. So far, the booby traps were keeping it pinned in and with the number of rounds that were being hurled at it there was a high probability that it was at least moderately wounded.

Ajax watched as Thatcher fearlessly plunged into the darkness of the building with his weapon raised while the other two skalds flanked the building. He could see the muzzle flash of Thatcher's weapon through the shattered windows, then elsewhere in the building thanks to the holes blown into it by Ford's panicked assault. None of the warriors outside dared fire for fear of hitting their commander, so they covered the building as much as possible, hoping that they could maintain a line of fire on every avenue of escape. The sounds of pulse rifle fire and whining spines rocked the building as the two combatants assaulted one another in the tight confines of the building. A glorious running battle was being fought inside between the champions of their respective races, and somehow it was fitting that the details of it were lost in the gloom of this tragic brackenworld.

From inside, the beast suddenly screamed in a way that Ajax had not yet heard. It was a high-pitched sound that yet somehow managed to rumble deep in his chest as if it were a powerful bass note. The very sound of it felt like metal nails raked down the side of a rusted piece of metal, and the pain was more in his mind than in his ears.

Grendel was calling for help, of that Ajax was certain, though why he knew this he could not understand.

"*Incoming!*" shouted Ford seconds before he fired bolt rounds into the sky, causing gory pieces of a shrieker to come splattering down upon the concrete.

Ajax looked down one of the booby-trapped alleyways on his left, just behind the building where Ford was positioned, and saw several ripper drones rushing headlong through it. The drones hit the tripwires without so much as pausing and two explosions tore them to pieces.

The det-putty had been packed with bits of metal and concrete that the marines had chipped off the buildings.

While the shrapnel was certainly deadly, the explosives had been set up to be easily spotted to direct Grendel's path. The drones proceeded, heedless of the obvious danger, and in the tight confines of the alleyways the concussive damage of the explosions killed them an instant before the cloud of shrapnel tore their corpses to ragged bits.

"It's calling survivors to it, the stragglers from other broken swarms," breathed Ajax in disbelief, forgetting for a moment that he held a rifle at all as he watched another pair of ripper drones willfully hit tripwires across the street, rocking the plaza with another bloody explosion.

"Ajax!" cried Rama as the marine slammed his good shoulder into Ajax, sending them both sprawling to the ground just in time to avoid being struck with a stream of burning death from above.

The shrieker spread its leathery wings, attempting to pull up and swing around for another pass, but one of the skalds swiftly shot it from the sky. Ajax rose to a kneeling position and fired a bolt through the chest of a ripper drone that had pushed through the carnage of the wrecked alleyway, suddenly realizing Grendel's plan. The beast was using the lives of its own kin to exhaust the killing power of the traps, giving it multiple avenues of escape. The signature report of a sniper rifle sounded and another shrieker smashed into the ground, reminding Ajax that the sniper was out there doing his best.

No sooner had the thought occurred than Grendel came crashing through the third and top floor of the building, showering the plaza with concrete and metal debris as it emerged. It landed with a sickening display of dexterity and seconds after regaining its balance, the creature lashed out with its barbed tail to strike a skald unfortunate enough to be nearby. The commando's body was transfixed by the huge barbed blade that protruded from the end of the creature's serpentine tail.

With a powerful undulation of its body, Grendel heaved the skald through the air towards Ford, who had already fired once at it and missed. As the skald's body flew towards the marine atop the building, the beast vomited forth another pointed projectile.

This time it did not miss.

Rama grunted as his body was speared by the whining round. By the time his corpse hit the ground, the marine's entire torso had been melted away, reducing him to a haphazard pile of sizzling limbs with a detached skull.

Ajax raised his rifle to fire upon Grendel, but was forced to readjust his aim as another ripper drone charged him, its comrades having given their lives to plow through the last of the booby-trapped pathways. Ajax squeezed the trigger of his pulse rifle and punched two bolt rounds through the ripper drone, blowing it neatly into three pieces of lifeless meat. More shots rang out and Ajax turned his entire body, sweeping the barrel of his pulse rifle around to reveal the last skald ignoring the two ripper drones that were coming up behind him in favor of focusing his fire on Grendel. Hart's rifle boomed in the distance as the sniper put down both attackers in rapid succession.

Ajax saw the creature slithering behind the low wall opposite him, the only bit of cover between him and the beast other than the ancient windmills. The creature spat a spine round in the direction of the skald, who shouted in pain, though Ajax did not see what became of him, intent as he was on engaging the creature himself.

Grendel screamed again, this time the psychic force of it causing Ajax to stumble a moment before he regained his balance. Above him, Ford was firing continuously, as was Hart, and Ajax knew that more of the scattered survivors of other broken swarms were converging on this plaza. The green flares Hart had sent up were no doubt drawing rifles to them as well, though Ajax was positive that this fight was going to be over, one way or the other, before reinforcements arrived.

As he and Grendel circled each other they kept to the outside of the low wall that encircled the windmills, exchanging blistering fire at near point blank range. The beast was grievously wounded, that much Ajax could see despite Grendel's somewhat supernatural ability to remain shrouded in shadows or obscured behind cover despite its tremendous size. Whatever might have happened to Thatcher, he had given the beast quite the fight. The marine was becoming rather certain that his own bolt rounds would be relatively ineffective against the beast's reticulated chitin armor, and only a lucky round would find its way into the creature's flesh. He did, however, still have a stick of det-putty, which he swiftly slid from his pouch. The marine slid an activator pin into the top of the stick and held it firmly in his left hand, knowing that he'd have to get very close to make it effective.

Ajax unexpectedly saw an opening, or at least his instincts told him there would be one if he rushed to meet chance, so he surged forward over the low wall. If he could use the cover of the windmills and his rifle in conjunction, perhaps he could get close enough shove the stick under one of the joints in the creature's armor. A wound like that might not kill it outright, but it would certainly immobilize it, making it easier for the others.

The marine sprinted across the few meters of open ground between him and the windmills, cutting deep left and then right to avoid the deadly spines being fired by the beast. The creature suddenly sprang into action and slithered forward also, as if it had seized upon the desire to kill Ajax with its limbs instead of a projectile.

It was just as well, thought Ajax, as he sprinted towards his enemy with rifle in one hand and explosive in the other, they had an account to settle between them.

The enemies collided in the thick forest of windmills. Ajax jinked to the right to avoid a whining spine projectile that tore into the windmill blade just behind where he'd been. The fluids inside the splintered spine created a pungent odor as they burned through the metal of the old machine. He squeezed the trigger of his pulse rifle and tracked the beast's movements as it slithered through the tall devices. Ajax wasn't so much trying to hit the beast as he was direct its movements to the left, and his ploy worked as the monster sped away from his hail of bolts. He felt, more than heard it coming up behind him, and spun on the balls of his feet, going to one knee, swinging his rifle around tightly across his chest as he did.

Grendel's barbed tail cut through the empty air where his chest had been, and the kneeling marine cut loose with his pulse rifle. Bolt after bolt slammed into the creature's chest and abdomen, most of them bouncing off the creature's body armor, though several did seem to tear away pieces of chitin and flesh. The beast continued forward despite the heavy blows it suffered from his pulse rifle. Ajax saw something pointed emerge from the beast's thorax, just beneath its slavering and distended jaws. At this range, he could see several pairs of smaller bladed appendages, reminiscent of the ripper drones, all of which lashed out at him as the beast was upon him.

The scything blades sheared his rifle from his grasp as a meter-long proboscis erupted from Grendel's thorax and thrust itself at his face. The marine jerked his head to the side at the last second and the appendage missed him by mere centimeters.

Heedless of the chitin blades that sliced deep cuts into his thighs and shoulders, the marine pushed forward. With one hand, he held the snout against his shoulder and with the other he jammed the det-putty stick into the slimy folds of the fleshy thorax from which it protruded.

The creature thrashed wildly and the blades of its smaller limbs sliced at the marine's armor. The creature couldn't get much momentum considering how close together they were, but searing pain in several places on his body made it clear to Ajax that he'd been wounded.

Ajax spit up bile and blood as he found himself face to face with the beast, its eyes once again threatening to lull him into numb inaction.

Then he roared, pulling his arm from within the folds of Grendel's thorax. As the marine's hand came away, he twisted his body with all his might and shoved his slime-covered forearm into the base of the proboscis. The activator wire was still gripped tightly in his fist, and as he pulled it out of the stick the circuit inside the det-putty was completed, causing the incendiary substance to detonate.

There was a wet explosion and Ajax was showered in gore as he was hurled through the air. The marine blacked out from the impact, coming to a moment later with his back against the inside of the low wall surrounding the windmills. His vision was blurred, though he thought he could see a pale serpentine shape disappearing into the gloom, taking the bone on bone sound along with it.

Ajax couldn't feel much of his body, and as he struggled mightily to turn his head to the side he could see that pools of dark blood were forming underneath him. As the darkness threatened to swallow his consciousness he could hear the booming sound of Hart's rifle. He hoped that the sniper was making good on whatever opportunity Ajax had bought with his life.

He flexed his fist and to his surprise he not only felt the movement, but realized that he held something in his hand. Ajax struggled to open his eyes, the lids feeling as if they weighed a metric ton. To his dismay, he saw that in his mangled right hand he clutched Grendel's proboscis. He dimly recalled hearing something about thanes and monsters in Thatcher's story, but the thought slid away before he could grasp it as his awareness faded into darkness.

NO EASY DAY

There were no dreams this time. Only pain.

Ajax fluttered his eyes open, his pupils struggling to cope with the bright lights being shone in them and gradually became aware of the scent of disinfectant. The marine flexed his fingers, and when neither rifle nor enemy appendage met his grasp, he bolted upright with eyes wide and gasping breath. He was in the medic station on Heorot, not the body forge as he had expected.

"Welcome back, brother," said the unfamiliar voice of a skald. His name was Wallace according to the name stenciled upon his chest plate. The skald put his hand on the marine's chest to keep him from leaping out of the med-rack. "We almost lost you."

Ajax groaned as the sniper helped him sit up the rest of the way. It wasn't until the man gently moved the marine to his feet that Ajax realized he even could stand.

"I didn't die," said Ajax flatly, as if he could not yet believe he'd survived his encounter.

"Re-growing muscle tissue and a few organs are medic level basics, comrade. Jarl Mahora and myself decided your turnaround time would be faster here than a mercy slaying and a trip to the body forge, but don't be disappointed," assured Wallace as he helped Ajax move from the rack to a small water basin where he could wash the sleep from his face, "We have quite the mission planned, so it's likely before this is over you'll die again, marine."

"Did we stop Grendel?" asked Ajax as he changed out of his sweat soaked medical scrubs and stepped into the shower tube. "Kill, capture, or otherwise?"

"It was a valiant attempt by all involved, though sadly, Grendel remains at large," said Wallace in a dejected tone as he leaned against the wall and patiently waited for Ajax to finish. "You, Ajax, did succeed in removing its proboscis. Initial reports from our labs on Crimson

Shard reveal a match between the secretions on the appendage and those left in the wounds of Grendel's victims, including yours. This information may prove to be a victorious discovery in the long term, and worthy of the price paid to obtain it."

"Grendel consumed Thatcher, didn't it?" asked Ajax, pausing in his process as if waiting for confirmation of something he already knew was true.

"Skald Thatcher did not survive the encounter, and it seems he suffers from the same condition as the Watchman," stated Wallace, who let his hand stray to his belt, where he fingered absently at the trench spike that hung from it. "I was his second, so have assumed command. Which left a hole in the ranks that I have chosen Hart, your sniper, to fill."

"High time he got a promotion, but Thatcher, it's hard to believe he fell. Was that rumor about the crew from Armor One true, too?" asked Ajax as he lathered up and rinsed with the swift precision that soldiers generally possessed. "It would explain how easily the Garm reached our walls."

"Yes, the enemy has certainly gained the upper hand, and in the process laid low two of our greatest leaders, with several dozen marines besides," answered the skald in a dark tone. Even through the steam of the de-con shower, Ajax could pick out the tinge of shame in the warrior's voice at being continuously bested by the invaders. "They have destroyed half of our working chain-fires, bloodied Armor One, and all but pushed us out of our trenches and behind the walls of Heorot itself. The situation is dire indeed, we are losing this war."

"Thatcher," grumbled Ajax as he stepped out of the shower and began sliding into one of the standard body gloves. "That's as bad as the Watchman, worse maybe, considering that he was special operations."

"With the skald's mind in the belly of the beast, combining with that of the Watchman, there is likely no stratagem or war trick we might hope to achieve that the hive mind cannot anticipate at worst or counter at best," nodded Wallace. "Chief Medicae Idris reports that the body forge is struggling to keep up with the casualty rates, and every available scrap of useable organic material is being funneled to the Bright Lance.

He needs time that the swarm will not give us, so I have pressured Command to make a desperate gambit in the hopes that a wantonly reckless stratagem will give us some manner of edge against an enemy that knows us so intimately. Thatcher was never a gambling man, though I am, perhaps that nuance will yield some advantage in the battles to come."

"What is the mission? I assume there can't be much time until the next swarm descend upon us," asked Ajax while he slipped on his boots and made ready to leave the chamber. "They may have lost countless thousands of organisms, but with two hive ships pumping out broods it won't take long for them to come back."

"Command has agreed to allow Jarl Mahora to lead three marine companies into the wastes alongside what's let of Armor One, to seek out and assault the hive ships," said Skald Wallace, his words stopping Ajax in his tracks. "The thinking being that if we attack before they are at full strength perhaps we can sufficiently forestall the next expedition against Heorot."

"Once we pinpoint the hive ships why doesn't the Bright Lance bombard them from orbit? We should just scorch the planet and call it an acceptable loss," said Ajax with some incredulity, "Or at the least launch starfighter sorties against them, if the atmospheric conditions are problematic for the void rounds."

"Ajax, this fight isn't just about killing Grendel, if that was the only concern, then yes, Bright Lance could just turn that whole sector into molten slag. This isn't a core urban planet like Titannicus, so the collateral damage would be minimal," responded Wallace as he stood away from the wall. "We are studying them even as they are studying us. The siege of Heorot isn't so much a meal for them as it is a weapons test.

Imagine if we were facing down hundreds of such creatures, each one able to fight and evade as this single beast. We must learn why there is only the one, and to find that knowledge we must enter the hive ship."

"You speak as Thatcher did, sir, all plots and feints and countermoves," observed Ajax, folding his arms across his chest and looking at the skald intensely. "Tell me, other than legions of marines stumbling around in the dark begging for an ambush, how are we to find the hive ships on this trackless waste of a planet?"

"The secretions on the proboscis you tore from Grendel's body contain powerful neurotoxins, presumably to help the beast immobilize the target and remove the brain matter," answered Wallace, "However there are cells within the secretion that emit electrical pulses which read just like brainwaves. They match up with what Command already has on file for the WarGarm, and it's thought that this 'transmitter cell' is what allows the WarGarm to, in essence, control the other broods, all of whom are filled with 'receiver cells'. What sets Grendel's apart is the power of the pulses and the density of those types of cells."

"I have a feeling you're going to tell me why this relates to us finding the hive ships. Cut to it skald, sir" snapped Ajax, the terrible knot in his stomach tightening as his mind raced with guesses as to what Wallace would say next. Each scenario was more grim than the next, and all of them seemed centered around him, otherwise why would such a high ranking operative spend so much time explaining the complexities of war and alien biology with a common rifle grunt. "The suspense is killing me faster than the Garm."

"Each time we resurrect the men who have been slain by Grendel's proboscis they die again moments later of severe brain hemorrhaging," said the skald as he continued to finger his trench knife, the burden of command perhaps resting uncomfortably upon his shoulders. "Command thinks those transmitter cells, when combined with the neurotoxin, are able to re-program something in the men's DNA. Upon resurrection, their brains generate receiver cells despite the fact that our body forge doesn't have the ability to create them. How exactly this is happening we don't know yet, but effectively, Grendel is altering the genetics of its victims, making them impossible to resurrect. Once it harvests the brain, it seems, for lack of a better way to describe it, the victim's mind belongs to the swarm. Each time they're brought back the men's brains are overloaded with information coming from the swarm and they die."

"Those cells are inside me, aren't they?" asked Ajax. "They're in my brain right now, receiving." He had to struggle not to let his knees buckle and collapse into a nearby chair.

"Yes," nodded Wallace reluctantly, before adding, "And they are also transmitting. You and Grendel are, in effect, engaging in subconscious communication with each other all the time. The beast was unable to harvest your brain. Whatever process of DNA transmogrification occurs never fully happened to you. As it stands, you are the only marine to be pierced by the appendage and not be harvested, but the poison and the cells got into you all the same, and both kinds of cells come back with you each time you are resurrected."

"The dreams, yes, the dreams," Ajax interjected. "You know I dreamt about the windmills, and then something similar happened in District 10," he added hurriedly, his mind racing over the events of the last few weeks. "We keep fighting in my dreams, hunting each other, and my wife, *gods*, my wife."

"I've read all the debriefings, Ajax, no need to re-live them now," said the skald, placing a hand on the marine's shoulder. "The point is, we have a theory about what's going on here, and how to put an end to it. Whatever they're developing can't be allowed to progress past its current stage of evolution. Biology is a messy business, and no doubt the Garm will, in time, correct this oversight. Soon, victims of Grendel will not share this connection with the beast. A simple tweak of the chemistry and the advantage you provide us will be gone, so we must use it while there is still time."

"I've seen the Grendel's hive ship, in my resurrection dream, the same one with the windmills," realized Ajax suddenly, coming out of his fugue once he understood what Wallace meant about turning his misfortune into an advantage. "Get me a topographical map and I know I could spot it, faster even if you had any municipal agri-maps for the windmill installations."

"The maps are waiting for you in the briefing room," nodded Wallace, who then turned to leave, gesturing for Ajax to follow him. "Our plan is a good one, but hinges upon you pinpointing the location of Grendel's hive ship. The others matter only in that they will be lending swarm support to our true enemy."

"What happens once we are in the hive ship?" questioned Ajax as he followed the skald through the medic station and, presumably, towards the briefing chamber.

"Who can say?" asked Wallace, who had seen more of the universe than Ajax. "We must lay eyes upon the birthplace of the beast, stare into the womb of Grendel's mothership, and learn what we can before we purge it from existence."

"And with the swarm working to recover and replenish the ranks after such a costly fight against the walls, now is the best time to press an attack," observed Ajax, feeling slightly sharper and more aware than he had upon waking, the painkillers finally wearing off and his limbs crackling to life. "Especially with Grendel wounded so badly, it may have retreated to the hive ship for healing or to have the appendage regenerated."

"Now you are catching on," nodded Wallace, "There is a natural revulsion felt in humans when faced with the Garm, a raw and primal reaction that reduces our critical thinking and pushes us into a siege mentality. Would you believe me if I told you that Command is beginning to suspect that this reaction in humanity is, in some way, intentionally exacerbated by the psychic force of the hive mind?"

"Like it wants us to dig in?" asked Ajax as they continued towards the briefing chamber. "Seems like we are rather skilled at siege war from my perspective."

"We very much are, and yes, it is the most effective way of combating the Garm in the main," agreed Wallace conversationally, giving Ajax the impression that the skald was happy to have a sounding board for his musings. "Yet we fight from our ditches and rarely think to counter. We tell ourselves that we are re-building, re-arming, and preparing for the next wave, and that the strategy of breaking the enemy's strength upon our walls is the best and only way to conduct our war. It seems like an acceptable stratagem, and has allowed us to all but halt their advance into human space.

However, with the new tactics and monsters we have seen here, there is indication that the hive mind is moving towards a shift in the balance of power. We must prevail, Ajax."

"We will, sir," affirmed Ajax with a certainty that felt false, though he did his best to master his fear and growing sense of unease. He was still silently reeling from learning that he carried within him parts of Grendel's cellular structure. Having such an immediate physical link with the beast made him sick, knotting his stomach even tighter, and he wanted nothing more than to take the fight back into the enemy's teeth.

"Fighting fit, marine?" asked Jarl Mahora in his gravelly voice as the skald and Ajax entered the briefing chamber. Mahora and two other jarls waited in the chamber alongside a group of seven skalds, with Hart numbered among them. The sniper gave Ajax a curt nod and the marine took his place near the projection table. Wallace keyed in his access code and several three-dimensional maps sprang to life in the air above the table.

Ajax ran his eyes across the maps, then at the schematics of a mobile fortress construct, and finally, at the task force breakdowns. His eyes went wide when he finally grasped the full scope of the skald's plan.

"Ah, you see it now, marine?" growled Mahora with a wicked smile, "It'll be bloody business indeed."

INTO THE NIGHT

Ajax fingered the torc that encircled his neck, both the symbol and the power of the Einherjar Corps, and closed his eyes. He allowed the clamor of readying for battle around him to dim in his awareness, removing himself from the hustle and bustle of the armor bay as hundreds of crew scurried about. They had good reason for it, for today it was humanity that was on the attack. It was always the Garm on the offensive, and Ajax found himself nearly overcome with bloodlust at the thought that today it would be the Einherjar who came first for the fight. Ajax caught himself then, noticing the aggression in his thoughts, the barely contained frenzy that felt so potent it could burst from his chest at any moment.

"We are both a step closer to the Blackout my friend," said Yao, who stood next to Ajax. The marine absently rubbed his throat as if recalling the sensation of the trench spike driving through him. "I can feel it beginning to encroach upon my awareness, influencing my thoughts."

"Meditation helps," growled Boone as he strode past the two marines to make his way towards the formation of infantry that was taking shape near the massive battle tanks.

"Tank crews mount up!" echoed a resonant voice through the deck channel, filling the earpieces of everyone with the certainty that battle was soon to be joined.

Ajax opened his eyes and watched as one hundred and twenty Einherjar crewmen filed out of the briefing chamber and flooded the deck. They were dressed in simple body gloves like those worn by infantry, though each was marked with the symbols of the tanks to which each crew belonged.

The heavy battle tanks were all named after various heroes and villains from old Norse mythology, in keeping with the Einherjar military tradition, and housed a crew of ten men each.

It had been some time since Ajax had been so close to the mechanized war machines, having spent most of his last several lives fighting in the desperate and bloody trench warfare for which Hydra Company had been created. Usually, the tanks were racing across the battlefield to support breaches in the perimeter, or using their heavy guns to pound the enemy with artillery fire. They had mounted weapons based on the same technology as the pulse rifles of the marines, only much larger, and far more devastating upon impact. A single round from the massive pulse cannon could slag an area several meters in diameter.

Jarl Mahora exited the briefing chamber behind the last armor crew and began striding towards the infantry unit that was gradually forming among the chaos.

Hydra Company had already been briefed, and so strong was their motivation to get some payback for the bloody street-fighting in Heorot, that most of them had arrived several minutes before their call-time. It would take Armor One nearly half an hour to run their full pre-battle diagnostics, weapons tests, and get the green light to proceed. When the jarl saw Ajax, he turned his attention to the pair of marines and walked over to them.

"Well, the tankers aren't excited about running escort for a bunch of construction trucks, but they'll take whatever piece of the Garm that command is willing to grant them once that part is done," snarled Mahora as he joined the marines. He swept his gaze across the deck to take in the sight of the tanks, trucks, and gathering infantry company. "After the horror show of days' past, I think they're eager for some payback."

"That's only because they have several tons of armor between them and the rippers," scoffed Yao as he rubbed his throat again. "I know when a tank goes down it goes hard, but come on, the average marine has resurrected more times than a whole tank crew put together."

"That might be true, but as we run out of parts to keep these things running there are fewer machines for the tankers to crew," added Sharif as he joined the other marines on the deck. "So only the best of the best still has a place on the rigs. There's a reason Armor One is so badass."

"Well, they're certainly going to get what they asked for," nodded Jarl Mahora before he slid his helmet over his head and buckled it into place. "You marines only saw the maps of the build site in the Hydra briefing, these boys just got shown the bigger picture, and it's a target rich environment."

Ajax was relieved that he had not been required to perform any of the briefing, only to consult before official word was given and troops began to file in. It was the memory of his resurrection dreams that had directly controlled the mapping of the mission. At last he was back to being just a grunt, as Skald Wallace and Jarl Mahora focused their attention upon the complexities of the mission, allowing Ajax to focus on rifle and trench spike.

Jarl Mahora gestured for the marines around him to follow, and they fell in step behind him as Mahora moved to join the rest of the infantry ranks massing on the deck. All of Hydra Company, as well as the marines of Manticore and Gorgon, had been briefed on the peculiar tactics and complex stratagems displayed by the Garm swarm they had fought in the trenches outside the walls and on the streets of Heorot itself. Plenty of marines had not lived to witness each new tactic with their own eyes, and it was important for the full body of soldiers to have a keen awareness of everything.

The Einherjar had found themselves facing down multiple instances of Garm swarms displaying complex tactics on the battlefield. It was chilling, and the sense of dread had been palpable in the briefing room. That sense of pending doom had carried over to the deck, and though the tankers of Armor One seemed eager enough, the marines of Hydra, Manticore, and Gorgon Company stood in formation with a grim fatigue. Despite their desire to take the fight to the enemy, the long years of war were apparent in each man's posture.

"We're deep in the weeds, boys, without a Watchman and hunting a new kind of monster on its own ground," growled the jarl through the company channel as he commanded the attention of the formation. They all snapped to attention, returning from their fugue in an instant, as if the jarl's voice was a source of strength. "Best we proceed as if we don't know a damn thing about the swarm, makes it less likely they'll catch us being predictable. They say the Garm adapt, well, I say marines overcome, so let's show 'em they picked the wrong ones to mess with. Mount up, marines!"

Skald Wallace and Jarl Mahora had both given parts of the briefing to the infantry units, so the assembled marines knew the particulars of their mission. While all three units had suffered tremendous casualties during the defense of Heorot, most of them fatalities, all but Manticore was back up to strength for the coming mission.

The men of Manticore had lost their jarl, a victim of Grendel's hideous harvesting. The jarl's absence was conspicuous, as was the skald commander's silence when asked of the man's fate. Secrets were still being kept, and the bulk of the marines still did not know that the Einherjar's ability to resurrect was being directly threatened.

Resurrection is our greatest power in this fight, thought Ajax as he watched Boone, Sharif, Yao, and Rama board one of the armored personnel carriers that were stationed next to the construction trucks and equipment haulers, and the enemy seeks to rob it from us.

We live, we die, we live again, he intoned to himself.

While it took eighteen years to raise a human being from infant into warrior, the resurrection of a torc-bearing Einherjar took only a matter of days. Like the Garm, the forces of humanity could hurl fully-grown soldiers into battle with little regard for their survival. It had given humanity the edge it needed to halt the advance of the swarm.

Ajax wondered how many of them would be once again riding the carousel of death and rebirth before this mission was complete. The memory of the Watchman and the grisly death of Thatcher gave him pause, sending a chill up his spine. The Garm had found a way to functionally negate the Einherjar's resurrection.

That was the skald's big secret, it was now possible an Einherjar could potentially die for good and he hated keeping it from his comrades. The men had willingly accepted the skald's lie about the Watchman, that his unique perspective and intel about the events of the fight for Heorot and the larger battlefield were needed upon the Bright Lance. The marines had seemed taken in by the skald's presence, as Ajax was certain he too had been, and the prospect of taking an offensive action alongside Armor One and the skald commandos was a sufficient distraction for most of the grunts. None of them had actually witnessed Thatcher die, and it had been the same for the jarl of Manticore Company. The marine did not like the deception, it went against the code he and his brothers lived and died by, though he kept it as he was ordered.

Ajax took Rama's offered hand and stepped into the APC, taking notice that Hart, in his new skald armor, had also ended up in this rig. The scout sniper wasn't really friends with anyone, what little time he did spend in the company of the other marines was with Ajax and his comrades.

Hydra Company only had the one sniper, as was customary in the Einherjar military structure, so Hart had little in the way of other men who understood his unique experiences in the field. There was something of a mysterious quality about the sniper.

Ajax imagined that some of it was carefully cultivated, much like the skalds who had once followed Thatcher and now followed Wallace, though much of it was truly just how the man was. To fight the Garm alone, out there in the dark and away from fellow marines, was a strange thing indeed.

Ajax took his seat and strapped in. His own precious few minutes out in no man's land, hunting a beast he could not see and wasn't sure even existed, was enough to convince him that he did not envy Hart's promotion in the slightest.

As everyone was taking their seat, another skald mounted the vehicle, and being the last man in line, turned and closed the armored hatch before taking his seat before the door.

According to the old Norse culture from which they borrowed so much military nomenclature, the skalds were storytellers and keepers of knowledge. It made sense that the warriors who doubled as military intelligence operatives and deadly commandoes would act in that capacity for this dreadful future war.

The man's chest bore the name Omar, stenciled in black above a raven decal upon his chest, each barely perceivable against the matte paint scheme of his armor. The raven indicated that this man, Omar, was a psych officer within the ranks of the skalds, masters in the craft of psychological warfare, though in truth Ajax did not see how such skills would apply to battle against the inhuman swarms.

They sat in silence for a time, then the vehicle shook as the engines thrummed to life and began to carry them onwards. There were thirteen men in the troop rack, including the sniper and the skald, and everyone was silent as the vehicle rumbled into the convoy. Though none of them could see outside the armored womb of the APC, each of them knew that the convoy of troop transports and construction trucks would sweep in behind a vanguard of six heavy battle tanks. They would be escorted by the remaining tanks as the mechanized group moved towards the objective.

The convoy was moving swiftly, that much Ajax could tell from the amount of turbulence and kick in the ride, but even with speed it was likely to take nearly three hours to reach the rally point. Each man sat with his own thoughts, and Ajax found himself unable to shake a looming sense of dread that had taken root in his mind. He had always been a staunch warrior, as Mahora pointed out, and yet, ever since first being slain by Grendel in no man's land Ajax had not felt fully recovered or completely battle-ready.

It was almost as if the horrible creature had taken a part of him as it had Thatcher and the Watchman, or more accurately, had cast something of a shadow over a part of him, a pervading and self-propagating sense of futility in the face of the might of the swarm. The thought of the alien cells inside him sickened the marine. He wondered if there might be some basis in Skald Wallace's suspicion that the Garm hive mind had some sort of psychic effect upon the warriors of humanity. A force that crashed against the minds of their prey before the swarm reached them. Robbing them of even a small part of their strength was a gain for the swarm.

"Do any of you marines know the tale of Heorot?" asked Omar suddenly, after nearly an hour of silence as the convoy lumbered onwards.

"Some myth from ancient Earth," answered Sharif thoughtfully, "It's where command got the idea to call the new organism a Grendel."

"One could argue this whole business was based on that story," stated Hart flatly.

"The scout sniper has the measure of it," nodded Omar as he shifted his rifle from one hand to the other so that he could lean slightly forward, holding the attention of every soldier present. "Heorot was a mead hall, like a sort of fortress, where men would gather to feast and tell stories. One evening, a beast by the name of Grendel stormed the hall and slaughtered many of the men there. Every few nights he would return and take victims, and no matter what the warriors did, this beast could not be beaten.

In time news of this ongoing tragedy reached the ears of a great warrior called Beowulf, who came to Heorot with a band of his finest comrades. They stayed in the hall and that night, when Grendel came, he was met with a bloody battle and eventual defeat. They laid a trap for Grendel, see? They drew the beast into a fight he thought he could win in the usual way."

"Many thanes died in that fight," said Hart, surprising the rest of the grunts by being familiar with the tale, as most grunts just took the old Norse terminology of their military on face value without digging deeper, "And Beowulf himself is doomed before the tale is done."

"The Garm already have the measure of how we conduct symmetrical warfare, so we have to mix it up somehow, find a way to fool the hive intellect in a way that only human beings can," responded Omar, giving Ajax the distinct impression that perhaps the psychological operative was not meant to be a weapon used against the enemy, but that his skills were in manipulating his own comrades. "Unless the swarm has found a way to decrypt narrative structure, it seems a fine way to fight with some level of unpredictability."

"There was no Grendel in the swarm until we named it such," insisted Hart as he tapped a finger against the stock of his rifle. "And there was no Heorot until settlers were sent into the wilderness to build it. This world was claimed after the war with the Garm had already begun."

"I thought that myself for a time, that it was all a matter of convenient jargon and cultural appropriation from our planet's ancient Nordic people, and then your man, Ajax, here, severed the creature's limb, not unlike Beowulf and the taking of Grendel's arm. That is a more powerful event than simply naming a thing, as if now that we have determined we are living a version of the Heorot story, a Beowulf rises from the ranks to face the monster.

It was humanity that named these creatures Garm, an ancient word for wolf, and from that old Norse beginning rose we Einherjar. We are the chosen warriors who are slain and rise again, just like the poems say, and one has to wonder if the learned engineers of humanity would have ever thought to pioneer such technology had we not had the story of the Valkyries and Valhalla to guide us," argued Omar, pleasantly enough, as the vehicle rumbled onwards into the gloom of the brackenworld. "Stories may yet prove to have been our greatest ally in this battle against hive and swarm."

Hart looked like he was going to say something else but was interrupted by the chiming of the proximity bell, which was accompanied by the ambient lighting inside the metal womb shutting off and being replaced by track lighting that illuminated the exit path to the hatch. Suddenly everyone's company channel was flooded with chatter as Armor One made contact with the enemy, but something was wrong. There were no shots being fired.

According to Armor one, it appeared, unbelievably, that all of the Garm were dead.

"Thane Twelve, break off and investigate grid point 42257432, that looks to be the epicenter of whatever happened," said Skald Wallace in everyone's ear-piece.

As the driver moved out of the convoy, the APC lurched back and forth as it struck several obstacles and crushed them under the tread. Ajax was startled as he and the other marines rocked with the motion, then belatedly recalled that he'd seen the number twelve stenciled on the side of the vehicle they were riding in.

"Omar, I want visual and assessment in five minutes, back on the trail in ten," snapped Wallace.

"As you say, sir," said Omar through the company channel. He swept the other marines in the APC with his gaze. "You heard the man, we will disembark once Thane Twelve hits the way point. Rifles and grenadiers, pull security. Hart, you and I are on recon."

Moments later, the vehicle came to a halt, and no sooner had it stopped, then Omar opened the hatch and leapt out of the vehicle. The marines poured out behind him, rapidly exiting with their weapons at the ready. In seconds, the twelve marines had formed up into a semi-circular firing line that moved a step behind Omar as the skald commando took point.

Ajax was immediately aware that the obstacles he'd felt being crushed under the tread were the broken bodies of Garm organisms. As the marine swept his rifle over the area he realized that the barren ground was littered with the corpses of ripper drones. Since the creatures were already dead, he could take the time to really look at them and he noticed with surprise that not all the drones had the exact same anatomy. Several appeared different from the others. It was subtle, an extra layer of armor here, longer scything blades here, a slightly darker shade of fleshy pallor, but it was noticeable.

"Omar," said Ajax as he continued forward, taking note that nearly half of the corpses were different from the others. "Look at the bodies, there are two distinctly different sorts of ripper drones here."

"Aye, and they seem to have killed each other from the look of the wounds," stated Hart, kneeling on the rocky ground. He gently pulled back the bladed limb of one ripper drone to reveal that the appendage was buried nearly nine inches into the chest of another.

"Be sure to snap a few shots with your helmet-cam, Hart, they'll want to see that," ordered the skald as he continued onwards, flanked by Ajax and Yao.

Omar reached the waypoint and stopped where he stood, looking down a low dip in the somewhat featureless ground of the brackenworld.

Ajax moved to join him at the edge. The marine looked down and saw that a WarGarm had died very messily. From the looks of it, the WarGarm appeared to be of the usual breed, as odd as it was for Ajax to think of the Garm in terms of different groups. The WarGarm had been torn apart by ripper drones, as evidenced by the heaps of shattered bodies and shorn limbs that filled the ditch.

"They died in droves to bring this thing down," breathed Ajax while he took several photos with his helmet-cam.

"Why would they kill their own?" asked Yao, visibly shaken by the sight of such visceral carnage, moving his rifle nervously up and down the ditch, as if he expected one of the corpses to leap up at them any moment.

Omar said nothing, only staring in silence at the sight below.

Hart and the rest of the marines joined them in looking down at the carnage-filled ditch, and they all stood quietly for a moment. It was as if each man knew he was looking upon a fresh new horror beyond anything they'd faced, and yet completely unable to fathom exactly what it was they were bearing witness to. The swarm never suffered from in-fighting or factions, it was a single organism, or at least it fought as though it was.

As Ajax stared into the hollow, dead eyes of the creatures, he knew that something more terrifying and important than simple violence had occurred here and he wanted nothing more than to return to the modest safety of the APC. He'd been a warrior for a long time, fought the Garm on countless worlds, and yet here he stood, nearly petrified by knowledge he couldn't even fully understand.

"Enough of this, let's mount up," snarled Boone in everyone's ear-piece, snapping the marines out of their thoughts. "Skald?"

"Right, we have what we came for," nodded Omar. The group of soldiers turned on their heels and moved to put as much distance between them and the ditch as they could, moving in double-time without having to be told.

Once they reached the APC and the marines started mounting up, Ajax, bringing up the rear, could have sworn he heard the bone on bone sound of the Grendel. He spun and dropped to one knee, his rifle scanning the area behind him only to see a quiet field of corpses and the dull glow of a dying sun in the distant sky. There was little in the way of difference between day and night on this planet, but it was enough that Ajax could tell that dusk was upon them. He held his position for a moment, but when no enemy revealed itself, he turned and climbed aboard, shutting the hatch behind him and strapping in for the journey to the objective.

FACE TOWARDS ENEMY

Ajax took modest comfort in the feel of the rifle in his hands as it snarled to life. In seconds the hatch of the APC would open and he would hurl himself into battle against whatever terrible creatures defended the hive ship. Radio chatter indicated that Armor One had struck the enemy a grievous blow, all dozen heavy battle tanks having rushed the enemy position.

The marine's dreams had been rooted in truth, and the maps he'd helped build were at least somewhat accurate. The hive ship he'd seen in his dreams lay ahead of them somewhere in the gloom, and within it, hopefully, the wounded beast, Grendel. The marine thought it was a good plan, this blitzkrieg assault and hardened extraction point, even if the next phase of it involved his likely death. Perhaps his last if Grendel were to get the best of him.

The construction trucks and infantry units had swiftly erected a pre-fabricated mobile fortress, using parts and scrap hauled from Heorot. Before the creation of the Einherjar, these mobile fortresses were used as forward operations bases that could be erected inside enemy territory within a matter of hours. While they had a certain degree of vulnerability to artillery, as compared to the time intensive trench networks that defended static positions, the speed with which a hard point could be erected inside enemy territory was a potent quality. Within several hours, a small force could occupy the fortress and have everything they needed to form a base of operations for aggressive offensive missions. While these fortresses had proven effective in the wars humanity had fought with itself in the bliss of their ignorance before the appearance of the extinction fleets, they were essentially deathtraps when facing the Garm.

Human soldiers were not likely to throw themselves against well-defended positions in suicidal charges, nor were they likely to attack the base in such numbers that their corpses created mounds that others could climb up to breach the walls. Eventually, it was determined that the mobile fortresses were an ineffective tool against the Garm, and that despite the heavy amounts of casualties a garrison could inflict upon the enemy, ultimately, the entire garrison would be slain and the ground again lost.

The mobile fortresses, like so many other weapons and tactics of modern warfare, had been abandoned as the military of humanity began to regress by necessity. Wars were fought in rather close quarters, reminiscent of the Napoleonic era of ancient Earth, and it was only once these more primitive and casualty intensive tactics were combined with the Einherjar clone soldiers that humanity managed to halt the advance of the swarm.

While the Einherjar had not yet won any systems back from the jaws of the Garm, they had at least managed to hold the line. In this case, the fortress had been pulled out of the deep storage holds of Bright Lance and dropped planetside so that a rapid extraction point could be created deep within enemy territory. They had no idea what awaited them in the depths of the hive ship and it was likely that the survivors would need a swift escape with whatever valuable intel they could recover. The walls might buy them the precious moments they needed for success.

Once they were on the offensive, even if this was a likely suicide mission, they had little choice in the matter.

Such were Ajax's thoughts as the APC ground to a halt and the skald threw open the hatch. The swarm was successfully grinding away the potency of the military presence here, and unless some asymmetrical ploy gave humanity an advantage then the Garm would inevitably take Heorot.

It was this inevitability, this implacable advance against any obstacles that made the Garm such a terrifying foe. The simple act of going against them on the offensive was incredibly empowering, not just for Ajax, but for all the assembled warriors. It felt like they were *doing* something instead of cowering behind walls and in ditches waiting for the next wave to crash.

His senses, even shielded as they were by his helmet, were assaulted by a noisy rush of information. He could feel more than hear the deep thumping of the tank weapons as Armor One dove straight into the Garm battle lines.

The thick, opaque, atmosphere of the planet made it all but impossible to determine the exact location of the hive ships that had embedded themselves into the surface of the planet, like parasites burrowing into the flesh of a victim. However, command had accessed old survey reports that remained from when the planet was colonized some years prior to the evacuation. With help from Ajax, they had guessed the most likely location of at least the mothership that bore Grendel upon the blighted surface of Heorot. Ajax's dream memories had been almost spot on, and Armor One found a piece of the enemy in their sights.

Flares lit up the sky and Ajax could see the gigantic, building sized structure that was the hive ship. To him it looked like a sort of sickening egg sac covered in interlocking chitin plates, and at the base of it he could see several orifices that contracted and expanded to vomit forth scores of Garm creatures. There were divots in parts of the hive ship, and sprouting from them were the wicked muzzles of what Ajax quickly realized were weapons, as they either spewed caustic gouts of viscous fluids or launched clouds of thick barbs at the attacking marines and armor units.

By the look of the scant few Garm that defended the ground between him and the hive ship, it seemed that Skald Wallace was right about the broods needing time to replenish. It was estimated that, given what was known about the Garm, learned by hard and bloody lesson over the years of war with the alien beasts, it would take them several days to fully recover from the losses suffered upon the walls of Heorot.

While there weren't many individual Garm fighting to defend the ramparts, the defenses themselves seemed to be alive. The Garm had constructed, or perhaps excreted, low, semi-translucent walls of what appeared to Ajax to be hardened resin or mucus. Into these bio-barricades were set any number of meter long spines that were no doubt meant to repel any charges by the enemy.

It wasn't until a section of bio-barricade contracted and launched one of the spines out of the wall in his direction that he realized it had other defensive capacities. The marine threw himself to the ground only to hear the short-lived scream of a marine behind him.

Ajax rolled onto his back and saw that one of the last marines to exit the APC behind him had been transfixed by the spine, which had punched through his armor as if it was nothing. The man staggered for a moment and then collapsed while the APC churned up the rough ground to roll closer to the enemy as the chain-fire gunner opened fire.

"*Ajax, on your feet!*" shouted Rama as he ran past the marine, raising his rifle to his shoulder and pumping rounds into the barricade as he went.

The marine scrambled to stand and brought his rifle up just in time to see a battle tank score a direct hit on one of the hive ship's defensive batteries. The wet explosion rocked the ship, and it shuddered, whether from the pain of the wound or the force of the explosion Ajax couldn't tell, but it was one less weapon pouring death down on them.

The marine sprinted towards one of the slag craters created by hits from the battle tanks and leapt into it, knowing that it would at least provide modest cover from the multitudes of enemy projectiles and fluids that were streaking out at the attacking marines.

"If the plan was to come over here and kick the hornet's nest then I think we did it!" observed Rama as he set his rifle on the edge of the crater and snapped a few more shots at the barricades and the growing swarm of gorehounds and WarGarm that defended it.

"This one's for Andropolis! For Tarsis Prime! For Ulanti!" growled Boone as he took a knee just above the others next to the crater and started methodically launching grenade round after grenade round, emptying his cylinder while bellowing the names of lost cities and entire planets that had been consumed by the swarm, and then working swiftly to replace his ammo. "For Bashepolon!"

"I think we've lost Boone," observed Ajax as he joined Rama in firing at the barricade, taking notice that his bolts seemed to do more damage when he fired at the somewhat softer tissue surrounding the spines.

"This isn't about armor or lives, gentlemen," said Omar as he paused on the other side of the crater to fire several times. "Whatever it takes to get on board that ship. Marines, on me!"

Omar sprinted forward and the others followed as ordered.

"Boone, empty a cylinder on that section of barricade, right where the spines are!" shouted Omar as he pointed, and Boone was swift to comply, still shouting out the names of humanity's fallen.

As the grenades exploded they ripped apart the wall in a tempest of shredded mucus, broken spines, and shrapnel. Their way clear of enemy fire, at least from the wall, the marines rushed forward without fear of the spines scything through their ranks.

At a signal from Omar, the APC Thane Twelve plowed through the gap, widening it, and giving the marines cover as they finished their rush to the wall. The chain-fire gunner sprayed fire into a handful of defenders as the marines took positions at the rear and to the side of the APC.

The driver revved the engines, but the living barricades were actually regenerating themselves, binding the armored vehicles tracks and preventing it from doing much more than moving a few inches at a time. It was all the driver could do to keep shifting backwards and forwards to avoid being stuck permanently.

Ajax sighted in on a gorehound and put a round through its flesh, the bolt punching through it just beneath its shoulder and causing the entire beast to explode from within. He noticed, despite the fury of battle, that the gorehound had been one of the subtly different sort, and as he took a second look at the enemy, both the living and the dead, he realized that all the beasts he could see were of the altered sort.

Something about this hive had changed, made it different than the usual Garm breeds, and that set his teeth on edge. After putting down another gorehound he saw a WarGarm erupt from one of the infantry orifices in the hive ship. It immediately began unleashing its fury upon the marines, and in an instant its devastating weapon had dropped two good soldiers, who now lay on the ground, wracked with spasms and drying up from the many spikes puncturing their bodies.

"WarGarm on the right!" shouted Ajax as he fired upon the beast, knowing that his handful of shots were unlikely to do much to the beast, but knowing that his comrades would follow his tracers.

Sure enough, the chain-fire gunner took notice and swiveled his weapon around. With the combined fire of the mounted gun and the marines, the WarGarm collapsed in a heap of ruined meat, only to be replaced by another as the hive ship's orifice erupted once more.

This time the WarGarm knew where the main threat was, and it strafed the APC with its gun, slamming spikes into the thick armor of the vehicle and through Rama's face. The chain-fire suddenly stopped barking, and Ajax looked up to see that the marine operating it had also died in the exchange. Boone and Omar poured on the fire, but Ajax knew that soon the creature would be upon them.

Ajax scampered up the side of the APC and shoved the spike-riddled body of his comrade back down into the troop hold so that he could take control of the weapon. As the marine brought the chain-fire up he fired it twice, only to have it lock up, the former gunner having forgotten his heat venting discipline, leaving the gun all but useless.

Ajax looked over at the WarGarm bearing down on them and prepared for death, only to see the creature's head suddenly explode as a thick, high velocity projectile slammed into it. There was no doubt in the marine's mind that Hart was out there somewhere in the chaos, and he resolved to thank the man when next they met, on this battlefield or the next.

Another APC slammed into the back of the one Ajax was mounted on, causing the marine's body to whiplash for a moment before he was able to steady himself on the chain-fire. He looked behind him and saw that the APC driver had used his momentum to shove the first vehicle through the slimy gap in the barricade, but now that vehicle had become stuck as a result.

But there was an APC inside the barricades now, and Ajax was happy to take total advantage of that fact when he managed to get the chain-fire up and running once more.

The APC advanced, heading closer to the base of the hive ship, and the marines who had been fighting on foot used the armored vehicle as cover.

Bringing the chain-fire up, he pulverized one of the embedded weapons jutting out from the hive ship noticing just how grievously their wild assault had wounded the living vessel. From his vantage point atop the APC, the marine could also see clearly what a heavy price had been paid for their advance against the hive ship thus far.

Two battle tanks had been reduced to smoldering heaps of molten metal by the various caustic streams and macabre projectiles being vomited forth by the hive ship's defensive batteries. Several APCs had either been slagged by the hive ship or had been overrun by the continuous stream of defenders that spewed forth from the infantry orifices at the base of the ship. Broken and torn marine corpses littered the battlefield on both sides of the living barricades. Despite such heavy losses, here they were, at the very gates of the enemy's keep, and that, thought Ajax, was worth the price paid in Einherjar blood.

He aimed the chain-fire at an infantry orifice set higher upon the ship, determining correctly, that it was for the shriekers. When the swarm emerged, Ajax shattered their ranks with sustained fire from his mounted weapon. By the time he stopped firing to vent heat, most of the enemy flyers had been blasted out of the sky.

"Swarms from the other hive ships are advancing, less than a kilometer out," boomed the voice of Jarl Mahora suddenly, his warning coming loud and clear through the task force channel. "Armor One get clear of those defensive batteries. Screen against the other swarms, see if you can buy us some time. Skalds, get your fire teams into that ship!"

"I can't believe we're about to do this," breathed Yao from shadow of the armored vehicle alongside Sharif, Boone, Ford.

"Silas, get on that chain-fire and keep those batteries feeling the burn," commanded Omar from his position behind the APC, his voice crackling in the ear pieces of the marines and APC crew of Thane Twelve. "Ajax, get the Blackout ready for deployment."

As Silas scrambled up the side of the APC and took the controls of the chain-fire, Ajax did as he was ordered and descended back down into the belly of the armored vehicle.

At the front of the troop transport bay was the matte black stasis pod in which the Blackouts were held. Normally, there would be at least two, if not three, minders to properly deploy the frenzied warrior, and Ajax had never attempted it alone. The APC rumbled along as the driver pushed forward, bringing the armored vehicle closer and closer to a large infantry orifice.

Ajax had no idea how many other vehicles would manage to successfully insert their deadly cargo, but he knew that even one of the fearsome death marines would cause enough havoc inside that the fire teams could maneuver within the ship.

Ajax picked up one of the minder staves and primed the electromagnet on the tip before depressing the activator on the outside of the pod.

Inside stood a fully armed and armored Blackout, held firmly in place by banded restraints. He could see little of the man's face through the wicked helmet, though he could see that the man's mouth was moving, screaming of the carnage he would soon visit upon his enemies. It wouldn't be long before Boone was exiled to a pod such as this, to live out his bloody nightmares behind the armor of the Blackout, forever trapped in a cycle of madness and bloodlust. The marine jabbed the minder stave into one of the slots on the Blackout's neckpiece, and then with his other hand Ajax hit the release on the restraints.

Instantly, the Blackout surged forward, though how much of that was the warrior and how much of that was the sudden swerve of the vehicle Ajax could not tell. Outside he knew that the APC had slammed into the outer parts of the infantry orifice, and that he only had seconds to deploy the fearsome warrior.

The Blackout flexed its fingers and strode forward to the exit hatch. Only the minder stave and all the strength Ajax could muster kept the warrior from attempting to tear through the hull to reach the enemies that he knew were waiting for him.

"Blackout in position!" said Ajax.

"Deploy and then pop the side hatch so we can follow," answered Omar from somewhere outside the APC, and Ajax did as he was instructed.

With one armored boot, he kicked the release on the exit hatch and deactivated the minder stave's hold on the warrior. The exit hatch burst open and the Blackout leaped through the opening.

It was risky to have the Blackouts pre-armed and un-manacled, but Command had deemed it an acceptable risk. It was possible that some marines were immediately dispatched by their former comrades during botched deployments, but the hope was that enough Blackouts would be hurled into the hive ship to buy the fire teams the time they needed to search for what would soon become Grendel's tomb.

The Blackout's pistol roared as the warrior plunged headlong into the hive ship's interior. Ajax dared not follow just yet, for he had no wish to die from the Blackout's uncontrollable fury. Better to leave that for the Garm.

Ajax rushed to the other side of the APC just as Silas descended from the gun mount. They shared a nod and the two of them opened the side hatch, one pulling the lever and the other wrenching open the door.

Immediately Omar leapt into the vehicle and began marching to the other side, followed closely by Boone, then Ford. As other marines piled in, each moving across the length of the troop bay and into the hive ship, Ajax saw that Sharif was not among them.

"Sharif?" asked Ajax of Silas as the two of them fell in behind the rest of the fire team, each activating his pulse rifle and preparing for the horrors that awaited.

Silas shook his head and then went through the exit hatch.

DEATH SHIP

The marine's boots made a wet thud as Ajax landed on the other side of the exit hatch. He immediately swung his pulse rifle to his shoulder and peered down his iron sights. The driver closed the hatch behind Ajax, as was the plan, so that he could have a better chance of still being alive should any of the members of the fire team survive long enough to need extraction. The APC itself was wedged at a steep angle inside the infantry orifice, preventing the orifice from closing. Ajax walked over the broken bodies of ripper drones left by the Blackout's rampage and kept his rifle at the ready.

There was little known about the hive ship interiors, beyond cursory anatomical details recalled by soldiers in the field. Humanity's warriors had halted the advance of the swarms, but done little in the way of pushing them back. However, this was not the first time Einherjar had penetrated the hive ships. During the Siege of Andropolis a full legion of marines, twenty companies strong, had advanced through the broken city streets to seize a cluster of hive ships. It was discovered they were horrific in their simplicity.

The ships themselves served as little more than giant breeding chambers for the various broods that comprised the swarm. The true complexity lay in the genetic knowledge stored in the ship's central chamber. In each hive ship encountered to date, the central chamber held a massive pool of raw genetic material suspended in a sort of amniotic fluid which was pumped by massive organs into a vast circulatory system that fed the various breeding chambers.

The hive ships were merely one part of the hive mind's arsenal of bio-forms. The spaceborne vessels that prowled the void were far more complex. The hive ships, for the most part, were classified by Command, and used by the extinction fleets as mobile fortress organisms that could generate their own troop forces. They relied upon the initial few swarms to harvest enough useable organic material to

116

feed the breeding chambers and to pump out wave after wave of hostile alien lifeforms.

The level of fighting involved in trying to seize a hive ship inevitably left the enemy fortress so badly damaged it would perish in the battle and be unrecoverable. As with the greater Garm war, scientific study of the enemy was a haphazard affair, usually done in battlefield conditions, and the intelligence such activities yielded was inconsistent in its quality and usefulness.

Ajax and the marines followed in the Blackout's wake of destruction, but he did seem to be slowing down. The hallway they ran through was actually more like an umbilical cord than anything else, undulating awkwardly as if even the floors and walls sought to eject the interlopers.

The Blackout had carved and blasted his way through a swarm of ripper drones, his pistol taking full advantage of the narrow passageway, not unlike the trenches such warriors typically fought among. Soon the passage widened to reveal a massive breeding chamber, with scores of slimy chords snaking through the air, making the entire chamber appear to be something like a jungle made of fleshy vines. From the cords, like so many abominable fruits, hung sacks bulging with amniotic fluids and embryonic ripper drones in various stages of growth.

From where he stood Ajax could see that as the embryos grew they weighed the vines down until the sacks burst apart on the rough floor of the chamber. As they watched, a long vine did just that, and five embryo sacks were torn open, fully formed ripper drones bursting from the tattered remains, screaming.

It struck him as odd that as quickly as the hive ships could breed the swarms, there should have been a stronger defensive force to meet the forces of humanity upon the field. Yet, as he watched the five rippers rush towards him, he realized that the hive was spawning troops as fast as it could, hurling them against the marines in smaller waves as they were born instead of marshalling a larger swarm of real strength.

The hive ship was desperate, defending itself like a cornered animal would, much of its former cunning tactics gone.

The Blackout launched himself into the oncoming drones, his empty pistol falling to the ground so that he could swing his massive blade with both hands. In the blink of an eye, two rippers were in pieces at his feet.

As the remaining combatants tore each other to pieces, Ajax noticed that these beasts, too, resembled the new breed he and the others had seen on the way to the rally point.

Boone moved to fire his grenade launcher, but before he could raise it, Omar put a hand on the man's shoulder.

"Hold you fire, marine," said Omar in a tone that allowed for no argument. "Slaughter is not our mission. First, we find Grendel."

"Then I'll just kill 'em on the way back out," grumbled Boone as he shrugged off Omar's hand.

The skald did not react to the clear challenge, instead, he turned and began marching quickly down the ridged flesh of the passageway, that looked for all the world, like stairs in the spongy body of the ship.

Ajax and the others followed in silence, stepping respectfully around the ragged corpse of the Blackout, the warrior having died in the slaying of all his opponents. It took every ounce of discipline in Ajax not to take the opportunity to gun down the unprotected embryos that hung so near him.

Boone vented his frustrations on a drone that hatched just a few steps behind him. The beast was born only to die seconds later as the grenadier's pistol punched two neat holes in its skull.

Over the wet biological sounds being made by the ship itself, the marines could hear the muffled report of other fire teams fighting their way through the ship.

Ajax had no idea how long Armor One could hold back the other swarms, so they had to move quickly. Omar motioned for Ajax to join him at the slick membrane that divided the ripper drone breeding chamber from the network of passageways presumably leading off to other breeding chambers.

"We were lucky to have entered the ripper's chamber, other fire teams no doubt found themselves assaulting the birthplace of much more fearsome beasts. We must make haste," observed Omar, before turning to Ajax and standing face to face with him, "You take point, Ajax. Considering your relationship with the beast, I have a feeling that you will know where it hides. Let your instincts be a guide."

"Relationship?" asked Silas as he and Boone exchanged worried looks.

"Something we don't know, Ajax?" asked Yao, stepping up directly behind the pair of warriors at the membrane barrier.

"No secrets between brothers," said Boone, his voice carrying a hard edge. "What are we really doing here, skald?"

"There are confidential elements about this mission, gentlemen," answered Omar, turning and facing the men, taking care to keep his weapon pointed at the deck. "Ajax was sworn to silence by Skald Thatcher and Jarl Mahora, himself, in order to maintain the integrity of the mission."

"I've encountered Grendel in my resurrection dreams ever since it killed me, after the first assault on Trench 16," Ajax said suddenly, ignoring the angry look from Omar as he confessed to his battle brothers. "The skalds think that the beast and I share some kind of psychic link, it's how we found the hive ships through all the atmospheric interference."

"So what? That's no stranger than anything else we've encountered," responded Ford, "Why lie about that?"

"Comrades," Omar finally said, after a deep breath, "This monster has found a way to functionally kill us permanently. He looked at each man in turn as the implications of his statement sank in. "The Watchman cannot resurrect without dying moments after he is brought online, same for Skald Thatcher, the jarl of Manticore Company, and dozens of other Einherjar. We must find this thing, subdue it, and get it off planet for analysis. Command believes that Heorot was a proving ground for this beast, that this entire campaign has been an alien weapon's test, and if we cannot stop its evolution here, then such bio-forms may begin to appear on the prime battlefront."

The marines stood in silence for a moment, the betrayal of their trust by command resting heavy upon all their shoulders, and then Boone spoke.

"For Andropolis," growled the man as he thumbed off the safety on his grenade launcher, "If this dumb grunt's brain can give us an edge, let's fraking use it." Boone gave Ajax a shove.

"For Tarsis Prime," added Ford, a grim smile spreading across his face.

"For Ulanti," chimed in Silas and Yao simultaneously.

"For Basepholon," nodded Omar, and then he gave Ajax the signal to proceed.

The marine plunged through the thick mucus membrane that separated the breeding chamber from the passage network and immediately his senses were assaulted by a flood of information.

Marines were fighting Garm organisms in three directions ahead of Ajax, as the membrane opened to reveal three different passages. Ajax was certain that the one to his left would lead him closer to his nemesis, and he ran in that direction, holding his rifle to his shoulder and adding his firepower to the blistering combat ahead.

Rounds tore through the walls of the ship and the body of a gorehound as Ajax and his team joined with another unit. They were from Manticore Company, and only three of them had survived their journey through the gorehound breeding chamber. As Ajax and Omar marched over the bodies of the freshly slain, the other marines were compelled to follow them, buoyed by the confident purpose with which they strode.

Ajax tried to do as Omar had suggested and he strained to hear the faint and alien psychic whispers in his mind. He could not fathom exactly how he was doing it, but the more he focused on his imagination's impression of the Garm cells in his body, the more confident he was in the direction he was going. His awareness began to narrow as he plowed through the hive ship, his marine's discipline taking over his body.

Ajax was barely aware of the vicious fighting his body was engaged in, the recoil of his pulse rifle little more than a tapping on the edge of his consciousness.

Now that he was in Grendel's realm and intentionally open to the beast's presence in his mind, Ajax found that his awareness of it was almost suffocating. As he moved, his reality became indistinguishable from the resurrection dream, with everything taking on a fluid out-of-time-and-space quality. The only sure thing in his awareness was that he moved here, turned there, climbed this, and swam through that to pass into the central chamber.

And there it was, Grendel, the hideous ravager itself, coiled at the base of a vast pool of raw genetic fluid, as if it was bathing in it. The proboscis was nearly fully regenerated and Ajax realized that the creature had indeed retreated to the chamber to nurse its wounds.

The psychic presence of the hive mind, or at least what Grendel channeled through itself, was devastating. Ajax was forced to his knees by the impact of it, for no human mind was meant to cope with the vast nuance of Garm communication. His nose was bleeding and his ears were ringing, and Ajax realized how awful it must have been for the Watchman or Skald Thatcher when they first resurrected after having their minds stolen by Grendel. The sound of marines shouting and firing their weapons seemed lightyears away from him, and yet he felt as if he must cling to those distant sounds to prevent from drowning beneath the psychic waves.

It wasn't until Grendel screamed for aid and the UltraGarm tore through the walls of flesh that Ajax jerked himself free from the mental whirlpool.

The gigantic beast used its scything blades to rip through the thin walls of flesh that separated the central chamber from whatever passage or area the UltraGarm had been lurking. The hive ship shuddered from the grievous damage dealt to it by its own brood. The ground beneath Ajax heaved and the marine was thrown to the ground then scrambled to his feet as the sounds of battle came flooding into his now freshly acute senses.

Marines and Garm organisms were flooding into the chamber from multiple entrances and tearing into each other with apocalyptic ferocity. Ajax caught sight of the UltraGarm cleaving Yao and Silas into bloody chunks with its sweeping blades before Boone attacked it with his grenade launcher. Omar and Ford were fighting back to back as they kept ripper drones from pouncing on Ajax.

"*Do what you must, marine!*" screamed Omar, and Ajax gathered his legs beneath him, "*We are with you!*"

Ajax sprinted across the central chamber, ignoring the carnage all around him as he rushed straight at Grendel. He was dimly aware of other marines running with him, but his singular focus was upon the enemy and he paid them little mind.

A ripper drone attempted to block his way and was pulverized by rounds from someone's pulse rifle as the marine sped onwards. Enemies fell before him as Ajax and his comrades charged the objective, mowing down all resistance even as many of those who ran with Ajax fell behind, either slain or caught up in the fighting.

Ajax locked eyes with Grendel. Instantly, he realized that the city he'd seen in ruins during his resurrection dream wasn't something from *his* memory, but from Grendel's. There was rage in those black eyes, there was individual awareness beyond the hive mentality of the Garm. There was a sense of Grendel's personal ambition lurking amidst the chaos of the hive's endless hunger.

Grendel uncoiled swiftly, spitting a spine projectile at Ajax, only to be denied its kill as Omar hurled himself in front of the deadly round. The skald went down hard as Ajax started firing at the beast's tail and mid-section. Ford added his fire to the attack, and between the two of them they pulped much of Grendel's lower body. The beast had been horribly wounded in the fight for District 10, and only marginally healed before this battle took its toll.

Grendel screamed again, a mixture of pain, rage, and this time, fear. It spat another spine round, this time spearing Ford through the chest and sending the marine spiraling away as Boone joined Ajax, his pistol at the ready.

The two marines leapt across the pool of liquid and slammed into the beast, firing as they went and driving the creature to the ground. Flailing blades sheared away flesh and armor as the wounded beast fought for survival, all cunning gone from its demeanor. Ajax didn't know when he had started screaming, though as Boone and Ajax both attacked the beast they pushed their vocal chords to the limit with primal rage.

His pulse rifle was gone, and in its place, was his trench spike. Ajax shove the point of it under the base of Grendel's neck and wrenched the blade, working it back and forth and stabbing repeatedly. Grendel tried to spit another spine round, but missed despite the close range, and soon it could do nothing but bleed.

Ajax roared as he used his entire body for leverage and with a mighty surge of strength that came close to madness he managed to tear Grendel's head from its body.

He rolled onto his back and saw that he had been hideously wounded, while Boone lay still in a spreading pool of his own blood.

Omar appeared in Ajax's hazy sight, the skald having clipped part of the spine that impaled him away so that he could move, though it was still firmly lodged in his body. The skald was moving on stimulants alone, that much Ajax could tell as the commando injected both himself and Ajax with heroic doses of painkillers and combat stims.

"The head, we have to get the head back to Mobile Command," Omar shouted at Ajax, and the wounded marine nodded and tried to stand. He gathered the slimy remains of Grendel in his arms.

And they ran.

It was miles back to the extraction point, and that was assuming the swarms of the other hive ships didn't tear them apart before they reached it. Even if they did, would the walls hold for long enough?

This fight was far from done.

It was a running battle through the raw mess of the hive ship's inner chambers, and it was all that Ajax could do to maintain his grip on Grendel's massive skull. Men and beasts died all around him, and he was only marginally aware of it. All his thoughts, clouded by the combat drugs and grievous wounds he'd suffered, were bent towards reaching the exit, any exit.

He knew that the men who fell here would not remember what happened unless their torcs were recovered. It was standard battlefield procedure to recover them from corpses whenever there was a chance, but here, in this desperate chaos, there was little hope of that.

Someone ran next to him, firing his pulse rifle to clear the way of ripper drones and as the last one was blown apart, Ajax could see one of the APCs wedged into the aperture of a deployment tunnel leading out of whatever ravaged breeding chamber through which he and the surviving marines now fled.

Roars of ravenous beasts filled the space behind him, drowning out the sporadic gunfire of those marines who had attempted to escort Ajax out of the belly of the ship. He dared not look behind him for fear that he would find too few marines at his back to hold the horde at bay.

The unique sound of a sniper rifle cut through the din and Ajax saw that Hart had taken up a position on top of the APC. The sniper was working the action of his rifle with superhuman speed, aiming and firing nearly as fast as a marine could with a pulse rifle.

Below the sniper, a hatch in the APC opened and two marines leapt out, adding their fire against whatever horrors followed Ajax. The marine never slowed his pace and leapt through the open hatch to crash onto the deck of the armored vehicle and the hatch was slammed shut behind him. The other marine was presumably still out there selling his life to buy time for the driver to get the APC in gear and push the engine hard enough to dislodge the vehicle from the hive ship's membranes.

Ajax finally let go of Grendel's head, letting the massive thing slide wetly across the deck as the vehicle lurched back and forth. The marine fumbled his way to one of the gun pods and grasped the handle.

The gun pods were small, only firing pistol grade ammunition, but in high volumes. They were designed for use in just this sort of situation, where the APC was being swarmed with beasts at close range and in need of clearing itself some room to maneuver. The sights of the gun pod were filled with beasts and Ajax fired manically, swinging the pod back and forth to its maximum one-hundred-and-eighty-degree arc of fire. The other marine in the APC did the same with his gun pod, and the vehicle bucked wildly as it plowed through, who knew what, massed nightmares.

The hatch popped open and Hart fell through, a bright red wound cut through his chest plate, the sniper rifle falling in two pieces to the deck alongside him. Ajax stumbled away from the gun pod, but his knees buckled and he crashed to the floor. Hart slid a pistol from its holster and fired upwards, driving away what appeared to be a shrieker that was attempting to climb down through the hatch. Ajax managed to pick himself up and with the help of the other marine, whose chest stencil read Wayland, got the top hatch closed before any other creatures fought their way inside.

Wayland immediately knelt beside Hart and dosed the sniper with combat stimulants and Ajax limped his way to the driver's cockpit. The pilot displays showed that the swarms from the other hive ships had pushed through Armor One's screen and were launching a counter-attack. However, as Ajax looked closer, it didn't seem that the attack was so much focused on the marines as it was on Grendel's hive ship.

Something twisted in the marine's spirit, a tightening in his guts as much as his mind as realization of what was happening set in.

Ajax had to get topside.

He couldn't trust the instruments, had to see it with his own eyes, that much he knew to be true. Wayland was too busy trying to keep Hart alive, and the driver so intent on reaching the mobile fortress, that neither noticed Ajax climb up to the top hatch and open it.

The air tore past him as the APC hit its max speed. Despite it, Ajax removed his helmet, determined to look upon these events with his naked eyes, no augmentations from his helmet, nothing to filter what he witnessed.

The marine watched with a combination of horror and awe as tides of Garm crashed into each other. Defenders poured out of the ruined hive ship and were torn apart by legions of Garm from the fresh swarms. Garm against Garm, thought Ajax as he recalled the nightmare of intercene carnage he and the others had found in the forgotten ditch miles away in the trackless darkness.

There were deeper forces at work upon Heorot than Grendel alone, and Ajax could not suppress the involuntary shudder he felt at that notion. Nor could he stop himself from groaning with pain and a swell of chaotic emotion when he felt the hive ship die. He knew not how, but presumed some lingering connection between he and Grendel, which most certainly extended to the living starship itself.

He felt it at the core of his being, the chill of it spreading through his chest and threatening to make him vomit. How much of it was dementia from the continuous stimulants that kept him awake or the presence of the Garm cells he wasn't sure, but at any rate, he knew beyond a doubt when the hive ship had perished.

In spite of everything he had experienced, there was something almost majestic in the gigantic lifeform, and he found its death somewhat tragic in its own way, like a part of him had just died. Reason told him it was just the Garm cells whispering their corrosive madness at him, and yet, however fleeting it was, in the moment of its death, he felt he had an understanding of it.

Grendel's presence in his mind seemed to fade once the hive ship died, but so dramatic was the loss of it that he felt suddenly empty inside. Grendel's own kind had turned against it, and Ajax could not help but feel that it was the individuality of Grendel that the Garm hated so much. He felt it more than he thought it, reacting to the exceeding brutality of what he saw as the Garm destroyed each other.

For a moment, it seemed as if the Garm were so intent upon slaughtering Grendel's brood that they would leave the marines to their escape, though soon Ajax saw that it was a fleeting hope.

Armor One had swept in behind the line of fleeing APCs, a moving defense of the personnel carriers, and as Ajax placed his helmet back upon his head he saw the swarms muster. His helmet's augmentation allowed him to watch as the two swarms from the other hive ships merged into one, rallied by several WarGarm that towered above the horde. Clouds of shriekers sailed through the air in the direction of the marines even as the land swarms surged across the ground.

Ajax felt as if the eyes of the WarGarm were upon him, singling out his APC as containing the remains of something the Garm wanted to destroy more than they wanted to consume the humans that carried it. Apparently, the Garm cells were still active in his brain, thought Ajax, even if the potency of them and the direct link to Grendel were somewhat diminished. He could feel the psychic pressure of the WarGarm, the alien will that drive the hordes straight at him.

They were coming for Grendel's head, and if the marines got in the way that was just more meat for the breeding chambers.

WOLVES AT THE GATE

Ajax wasn't sure when he passed out, but when he came too he and Hart were being lifted on stretchers and carried away from the APC. He looked up and saw that the APCs had rallied in the motor pool at the center of the mobile fortress. Mechanics worked frantically on the more damaged ones, fixing treads, patching armor, and bringing chain-fires back online. There was a peculiar clanking noise on the other side of him and as Ajax turned his head painfully, he saw Jarl Mahora walking next to him. The clanking sound was coming from at least two dozen torcs festooning the jarl's belt, a testament to the casualties of the day.

"They're coming for Grendel's head, sir," said Ajax with a voice strained by exhaustion and pain, "All of them, right now."

"Aye, it seems they've learned how to kill each other. Maybe drank a bit too deeply from humanity's cup, eh?" growled Mahora, his grim expression all the darker for the gallows humor he seemed to find in the situation. "Well, don't you worry, marine, we're gonna hang it high so they know right where to come get it."

"FOB Thane was just supposed to be a rally point, this fortress isn't going to be able to repel that kind of attack," Ajax reminded his jarl as the medics continued to carry the stretchers towards the makeshift infirmary container, confused at Mahora's apparent eagerness to lock horns with the enemy again so soon after such a costly battle. "Seize Grendel and get it offworld, that was the plan."

"Certainly was, but that was before one of those new hive ships launched itself back into orbit," nodded Mahora as he gestured to the sky above them, and in the distant darkness of low orbit Ajax could see the impossibly bright flashes that were the telltale signs of a mighty void battle being waged in the heavens. "Seems like the Garm guessed our plan, cannibalized the hive ship that was damaged on entry to make the other stronger. If that hive ship manages to destroy Bright Lance we are stranded on Heorot and without a body forge."

"I'm ready, sir, just hit me with more stims and give me a rifle," rasped Ajax as he fought to lift himself off the stretcher, only to be silently pressed back down by the medic.

"You're a dead man walking, Ajax, you'd be a liability and you know it. Let the medics do their job, and if we can't hold the line I'm sure the enemy will come to you," scoffed Mahora warmly. "The Garm are throwing everything they have at us, and their hive ships are gone, so for them there is no reinforcement and without Bright Lance we have no resurrection. For once, we are on even footing with those bastards. If we win here, we win the planet, so we stay and we fight."

Ajax attempted again to rise, but he had not the strength, and begrudgingly allowed himself to be taken the rest of the way to the infirmary. Once inside he saw that the medics building was one of the prefab containers that formed the bulk of the buildings inside the mobile fortress perimeter. While the fortress itself was simply a massive square comprised of scaffolding, deck planks, and armored barricades dotted with gun mounts and firing steps, the interior was somewhat open. In addition to the infirmary he knew that there would be an armored munitions depot, a motor pool hub, and at least some manner of command bunker. He'd been part of the advance team so did not actually see the fortress being built, though from his training he could guess as to the details.

The marine did his best to stay conscious, but now that he was finally prone and out of immediate danger, he found it harder and harder to stay awake. A sudden darkness enveloped him, and somewhere in the distance of his perceptions he felt the prick of a needle. No doubt the medics had sedated him, which was just as well, as the stimulants were wearing off and being gradually replaced by pain.

There were no dreams, and for that, Ajax was thankful. When his eyes fluttered open his senses were assaulted with noise. What had awakened him from his drug and pain induced stupor was Hart sliding a knife through the restraints that had been holding Ajax in place.

"Apparently, your connection to Grendel has become common knowledge during our slumber," said Hart in a stony voice as he helped Ajax to sit upright. "The medics tied you down once you were out."

"I can't blame them," said Ajax as he willingly allowed Hart to dose him with stimulants, then rubbed his sore arm as the sniper dosed himself. Both marines were suffering from shaky hands, a palsy that was common when the combat drugs in their systems were near the overdose threshold. "We will both need to resurrect soon if we keep pounding the stims like this, the nerve damage we are doing is already starting to show."

"I don't believe that dying will be much of a problem, it doesn't sound like we're winning out there, and if Bright Lance is destroyed we will have lived our last. The medics have already abandoned us to join the defense," observed Hart as he pulled himself into a basic body glove and handed one to Ajax, who did the same. "We'll need to scavenge weapons from the dead, so be prepared to scramble, who knows what's waiting for us out there."

"Nothing we haven't faced before," said Ajax as he flexed his shaky fingers and limbered himself up as best he could despite his wounds and battered body before accepting a long scalpel blade from the sniper. "I'm ready."

The two men flung open the door of the infirmary and plunged through it. They were immediately met with a hurricane of violence, the sight of which shook even these hardened veterans to the core of their being. The motor pool was mostly empty of vehicles, the APCs that could function having presumably been sent out into the field to join Armor One in its rolling battle outside.

Across the square that was the fortress, marine and Garm corpses choked the decking and littered the open ground of the fortress proper. Marines fought each other as several of them screamed for meat.

Riflemen defiantly stood the ramparts and fired their weapons in all directions, alternating between defending the walls and taking out enemies that had breached the perimeter. One entire section of wall had been torn down by what appeared to have been a valiantly suicidal attack by UltraGarm, and judging from the many broken bodies in the breach it was a cluster of Blackouts that had sold their lives to plug the hole.

The sky was ablaze with falling debris and Ajax could see the rain of wreckage coming down from orbit, burning as it fell to the surface. Much of what fell was organic, and the smell of cooking alien flesh choked his nostrils as much as the sight of burning metal cascading chilled his heart. If Bright Lance wasn't dead, she was at least badly wounded, and would be no help here.

"Ajax!" shouted Hart as he pitched the marine a pulse rifle before racking the slide of his own to vent the heat that had shut it down. *"Eyes center!"*

Ajax checked his weapon, seeing that it had two thirds of a carbon mag left, following Hart's pointing finger with his gaze.

At the center of the fortress a long piece of sturdy rebar had been buried upright in the ground, and on the top of it, as if impaled by the spear of Odin himself, was the head of Grendel. Around the base of the pole stood three Einherjar, one of them Jarl Mahora. At their feet were piles of bodies, both human and Garm, along with many destroyed or discarded flak boards, and yet more of the enemy surged towards them.

Hart and Ajax leapt into the fray and began targeting ripper drones that had scaled the nearby walls on their left. The two men took a knee and fired with rapid precision, each venting after the tenth shot despite the adrenaline of what they assumed was the last fight of their lives. With the rippers down, Ajax turned his attention to a gorehound that had just blasted a marine off the firestep. Once the gorehound was dead, Ajax sought another target. An easy thing in this swirl of enemies.

Suddenly, the entrance to the fortress buckled from multiple impacts, and Ajax could hear the shearing of metal from the other side. The gate was reinforced and the strongest part of the fortress, yet, as the marine looked, he could see the last handful of defenders being slain by whatever was attacking from below. When a long spine sprouted through the back of a marine's neck, Ajax recognized the projectile as belonging to the fearsome weapons of the WarGarm.

"Einherjar, to me!" bellowed Jarl Mahora, and along with several others capable of doing so, Ajax and Hart sprinted across the open ground towards their leader. "Shieldwall!"

The marines did as ordered. The ten marines left to answer the call picked up the least damaged of the discarded flak board as the WarGarm continued to tear through the main gate. In seconds, the marines locked their boards together and held firm, each man certain that they were living their final moments. The enemies had all but thinned out as the concentrated fire of the marines mowed them down. Soon no more Garm came pouring over the walls. All that remained was the steady violence against the entrance.

"The swarm is spent," observed Hart from behind Ajax as the sniper set his flak board over the marine to protect him from above. "All that remain are the WarGarm and we seem too few."

"Wolves are at the gate, brothers!" roared Jarl Mahora as he beat the stock of his rifle against his flak board. "Show them how we die!"

Adrenaline surged through Ajax in equal measure to the combat stims as the WarGarm breached the entrance. The metal imploded from the force of a final impact. The marine could see that the Garm had used their corrosive projectiles to weaken it to the point that they could bash it down with their scything blades and mighty limbs.

As one the Einherjar opened fire, a tempest of rounds tore through the first of the WarGarm. They kept coming, and the marines kept firing, though after the second massive beast was turned to pulp, the others managed to spread out of the tight entrance and return fire.

A wave of spines slammed into the shield wall, several of them punching through the flak boards and impaling the marines behind them. The shieldwall held despite the many losses, and kept pouring on the fire. Without the advantage of concentrating fire on one beast at a time, though, the fusillade was much less effective. A wounded WarGarm was still quite deadly, and one that had lost one of its legs still managed to fire its caustic weapon.

The spray of globular projectiles melted away the flak board that Ajax was holding and burned through the body of the man standing next to him. It was only after the man fell in a smoldering heap that Ajax recognized the corpse as Skald Omar, having apparently survived the wound he took in the hive ship only to be cut down here.

There was little to do but fight on, and Ajax went down on one knee in the attempt to make himself a smaller target. He fired over and over, putting bolt after bolt into the wounded WarGarm, and as the tenth round threatened to overload his rifle, the marine's last shot put it down. Ajax threw his rifle aside and picked up Omar's, raising it to his shoulder and he continued to squeeze the trigger. There was no room left for strategy or tactics, only the bloody grind of close quarters violence.

Ajax did not recall when he swapped Omar's empty rifle for yet another scavenged weapon, and it mattered little. All that concerned him was that he found a piece of the enemy in his sights and kept shooting. It wasn't until his rifle clicked empty that he snapped out of his trance and cast his eyes about in search of another weapon.

Soon his hands curled around the grip of a pulse rifle still clutched in the arms of a dead marine. He wrenched the rifle away from the corpse and his ears were met with a unique clinking sound. Before he could look down to see what it was, a wounded WarGarm hurled itself at him, and sank one of its remaining scything blades through the meat of his thigh. Ajax knew instantly that his femoral artery had been severed, for without any combat armor to deflect or absorb the blow he'd taken the full force of it. The marine jammed his rifle into the dripping maw of the creature and squeezed the trigger. The superheated bolt burst apart the WarGarm's skull and showered Ajax with gore.

The marine fell to the ground, with his back against the pole topped with Grendel's head. Ichor seeped down the pole from the ragged mess and stung the marine's bare skin. He ignored the pain and trained his rifle on another WarGarm that, despite having lost what appeared to be its right arm and much of its shoulder, pressed the attack. Ajax selected full-auto fire and cut loose, spraying the enemy with rounds until the weapon overloaded and shut down. Thankfully, the already wounded beast collapsed before it reached him.

Ajax's perceptions swam and he knew he was bleeding out, there was no stopping that now. He felt around upon the corpse he'd seized the rifle from and his hands found the sidearm holster with a pistol still in it. Ajax looked down to check the magazine and in doing so realized he'd fallen next to the mangled body of Jarl Mahora. The marine was shocked at the idea of such a larger than life individual dying, then his eyes found Hart's body amidst the bloody tangle.

The marine blinked several times trying to clear the haze of his fading vision, only to find that focusing was all but impossible. He seemed to be the only thing moving in the fortress, and even he was slowing by the second. No Garm appeared to attack him, and no marine stirred among the dead. All that he could hear was the howling wind and the impact of void debris that still rained down from the burning sky. Soon even that dim awareness faded, and he sank beneath the waves of a cold darkness.

ONLY IN DEATH

Ajax dared not open his eyes as Rowan's hands caressed his chest, her scent strong in his nose as he kissed the space just under her ear. That was always the sweet spot for her, a fact that he'd often used to his advantage. He pulled her close to him in the darkness behind his eyes and pressed one hand against the small of her back, running the other gently up her thigh. Her lips found his, and her hands guided him inside her.

Rowan had died on Andropolis along with billions of others. It hurt him to acknowledge that fact, a brutal truth he avoided in his waking life. At least in his dreams, she was here with him, and that made dying something less to be feared and more to be embraced. It would always end, and he would awaken to the fight once more, but for now all he wanted was this heat and this darkness and her.

But it did not end.

Even after they lay panting in each other's arms Ajax did not awaken, and he began to suspect that he'd finally died his final death. Was this the release that he had secretly hoped for? No man was made to live and die in such an endless cycle as the Einherjar. The Blackouts were proof of that.

No Grendel stalking him. No terrible visions haunting him. Just Rowan. His wife. Did he dare open his eyes? What awaited him upon waking?

"Open your eyes, Ajax," whispered Rowan, though her voice now sounded distorted, and the marine couldn't tell whether that was because he was listening to her through something like water or if he'd just forgotten what her voice sounded like.

Initially, he refused, but she said it again, this time more changed and even further away. Finally, with a bitter acceptance, he forced himself to open his eyes.

The body forge.

Familiar faces met his gaze, and Idris welcomed Ajax back to consciousness.

Ajax was silent, it was all he could do not to weep, and yet he steeled himself as best he could. If he was alive and in the body forge with Idris that meant Bright Lance still flew.

"Welcome back, marine," said Idris with a smile that seemed at once exhausted and relieved.

"Hope you enjoyed your nap, Einherjar, you earned it. Heorot is ours again, but there's no rest for the weary," growled Mahora as he stepped into the light, "Grab your gear and report to the launch deck in thirty minutes, we'll debrief en route."

"Heorot will be secured by another unit from fleet," assured Idris in answer to the questioning look he got from Ajax as the marine moved his gaze from Mahora to the medicae. "We are being re-routed to the prime battlefront as part of a new initiative."

"Did the Garm break through somewhere on the front?" asked Ajax as he let Idris help him out of the forge.

"No, we still hold firm. Given the nature of events here on Heorot, the marines of Hydra Company and the rest of the einherjar here have experience with Garm warfare that no other units does," answered Idris.

"We have been assigned to something called Task Force Grendel," said Mahora with a savage smile. "I imagine we are about to start hunting monsters."

NO HERO YET

Ajax stood in the chamber alone, staring at the head of Grendel as it floated, suspended in thick preservatives. Even in death, he could still feel the psychic echoes of the beast, and in the distance of the cold void he knew that the hive mind was out there listening for him.

Bright Lance was en route to destinations unknown, and the marines aboard were preparing themselves to be deployed into some fresh hell.

Monster hunters, indeed, thought Ajax to himself as he and the dead Garm ravager stared at one another.

"If the skalds are right, and you really are Grendel," whispered Ajax as his hand strayed to the torc at his throat. "Then what dragons await us among the stars?"

Don't miss out!

Visit the website below and you can sign up to receive emails whenever Sean-Michael Argo publishes a new book. There's no charge and no obligation.

https://books2read.com/r/B-A-KCOJ-WHANC

BOOKS 2 READ

Connecting independent readers to independent writers.

Also by Sean-Michael Argo

Extinction Fleet
Space Marine Ajax

Starwing Elite
Alpha Lance

Standalone
War Machines
DinoMechs: Battle Force Jurassic

Milton Keynes UK
Ingram Content Group UK Ltd.
UKHW041815060923
428148UK00001B/45

9 798223 028192